"Highly entertaining . . . dry wit, on-point observation."
—*Newsday*

"A light-of-heart, kick-of-ass novel."
—*Elle magazine*

"A lightly literary tour de farce."
—*O Magazine*

"Ballsy . . . keeps us eagerly guessing."
—*Kirkus Reviews*

"A mischievous treat."
— *Boston Globe*

"Howl away with LAURA RIDER'S MASTERPIECE,
a madcap tale of a quest for literary success."
—*Self*

## Praise for LAURA RIDER'S MASTERPIECE

"An entertaining satirical farce."
— *St. Louis Post-Dispatch*

"Why this novel? Well, who wouldn't want a peek inside the mind of an aspiring romance writer who cuts off sex with her hubby, then engineers an affair for him so she can study it?"
— "The Must List," *Entertainment Weekly*

"An outstanding read...Jane Hamilton just keeps getting better: wiser, more dexterous, more entertaining with every novel...She creates for her characters rich inner worlds, wholly satisfying to encounter; a Hamilton novel amounts to a romp through a vast, rolling emotional terrain."
— *Toronto Globe and Mail*

"Jane Hamilton has written a sex comedy, and the world is a better place for it. LAURA RIDER'S MASTERPIECE is a densely observed and seriously droll novel that reads like a dream. Astute, brazen, and very funny, Hamilton has flexed all her muscles here, coming up with a kind of *Les Liaisons Dangereuses* for our rapid-fire e-mail era."
— Meg Wolitzer

*more...*

Also by Jane Hamilton

*When Madeline Was Young*
*Disobedience*
*A Map of the World*
*The Short History of a Prince*
*The Book of Ruth*

# Laura Rider's Masterpiece

---
A Novel
---

## Jane Hamilton

**GRAND CENTRAL**
PUBLISHING

NEW YORK    BOSTON

This book is a work of fiction. Names, characters, places, and incidents are the product of the author's imagination or are used fictitiously. Any resemblance to actual events, locales, or persons, living or dead, is coincidental.

Jenna Faroli would certainly have used Susan A. Clancy's book *Abducted* and Janice A. Radway's *Reading the Romance* to learn about persons who have had alien encounters, and about romance readers. I'm indebted to those authors for their fascinating books. Thanks, as always, to the Ragdale Foundation, and this time, thanks to Mr. Right of the *Isthmus* for the best line.

Grand Central Publishing
Hachette Book Group
237 Park Avenue
New York, NY 10017

www.HachetteBookGroup.com

Printed in the United States of America

Originally published in hardcover by Grand Central Publishing.

First Trade Edition: March 2010
10  9  8  7  6  5  4  3  2  1

Grand Central Publishing is a division of Hachette Book Group, Inc.
The Grand Central Publishing name and logo is a trademark of Hachette Book Group, Inc.

The Library of Congress has cataloged the hardcover edition as follows:
Hamilton, Jane
    Laura Rider's masterpiece / Jane Hamilton.—1st ed.
        p. cm.
    ISBN: 978-0-446-53895-4
    1. Triangles (Interpersonal relations)—Fiction. 2. Wisconsin—Fiction. Domestic fiction.
    I. Title.
    PS3558.A4428L38 2009
    813'.54—dc22                                                    2008010093

ISBN 978-0-446-53894-7 (pbk.)

*Book design by Charles Sutherland*

*For*
*Dorothy, Gail, and Karen Joy*

Laura Rider's Masterpiece

# Chapter 1

JUST BECAUSE LAURA RIDER HAD NO CHILDREN DIDN'T mean her husband was a homosexual, but the people of Hartley, Wisconsin, believed he was, and no babies seemed to them proof. They also could tell by his heavy-lidded eyes that were sweetly tapered, his thick dark lashes, his corkscrew curls, his skinny legs and the springy walk, and the fact that he often looked dreamily off in thought, as if he were trying to see over the rainbow. In the municipal chambers at a public meeting, a town councilman had once said that Charlie Rider needed a shot of testosterone. It was a mystery to Laura that in Hartley, population thirty-seven hundred, people who had never been to a gay-pride parade or seen any cake boys that they knew of outside of TV actors, were so sure about Charlie. She assumed that, like any place, the town was laced with fairies, not visible to the naked eye, but Charlie, she could testify, was not one of them. Laura herself had not been to a pride parade, but her personal experience included her flamboyant uncle Will, her outrageous cousin Stephen, her theatrical playfellow Bubby from the old neighborhood, and also Cousin Angie, who had tried to shock them all by having a lesbian phase in college. No one in the family, it turned out, cared.

Mrs. Charles Rider was the one qualified to set the residents straight about her husband, not because of her expertise with her various beloved queens, but because of her long life so far with the man himself. Make no mistake, Laura would have liked to say, Charlie Rider was crazy about women. Charlie was not squeamish. Charlie, if they must know, worshipped the pudendum. She wanted to lambaste the town, to tell them that the cruelty he had endured through his school years had been grossly misplaced. In the bedroom he was not only at the ready, always, he was tender, appreciative, unabashed, and, incidentally, flexible. A night with Charlie was equivalent, both for burning calories and in the matter of muscle groups, to doing the complete regime of the Bowflex Home Gym. Charlie emphatically was not fag, swisher, fembo, Miss Nancy, chum chum, or any of the other names he'd been called since second grade. It had always impressed Laura that a town that thought it had so few gays had so many labels for the aberration that was supposedly her husband.

The real problem was that, after twelve years of marriage, Laura had become permanently tired of his enthusiasm. She'd realized that if you gave an inch you were in for the mile, that if you were even occasionally available he assumed the welcome mat was always on the stoop. She disliked the whole charade of fatigue or preoccupation, but she hated, too, how the pressure of his need had jumbled not only her body but her brain. She was losing her mind, losing her ability to stay focused and organized. When he hung around her study after dinner, when his sighs seemed to blow through the house, she knew she'd have to give up her beautiful, well-thought-out plan for a productive evening. And for what? Come morning, there he'd be, eyeball to her eyeball, fresh, apparently, as a daisy, as if months, not hours, had passed since the last full-body slimnastic routine.

Both before and after she'd quit sleeping with him, she'd read articles and books about sexual fatigue. There were features in women's magazines, often with photographs of bombed-out wives, shoulders sagging, bags under the eyes, sitting on perfectly made beds. Laura understood that she was among millions, that she was another casualty in what was clearly a national epidemic. She had explained it to Charlie as kindly as she could, saying that, just as a horse has a finite number of jumps in her, so Laura had used up her quota.

"No more jumping?" he said. "Not ever?"

"I can't," Laura said. "I love you, but I can't."

"What if we take down a few of the fences on the course? Lower the bars? Shorten the moat by the boxwoods? How—how about trying a—"

"I'm sorry," Laura said, and in the moment she did feel a

little rueful. "Charlie, I am sorry, but can't you see? I'm out to pasture."

Her secret fear about this new phase of their life was that, without his one superb talent, which, she granted, had given her hours of pleasure and even, she would say, fulfillment— without that contribution to the household, she wondered if he actually had all that much else to offer, if he would prove to be worthless. What a terrible thought! She didn't mean it. But might he be like a quarterback who, once retired, didn't have the smarts to buy a restaurant chain or a fitness club? When such ideas, unpoliced, crept up on her, she strenuously defended Charlie to herself. He had a multitude of virtues: his help to her in their business, his sunny nature, his ability to make jokes about catastrophes, his flights of fancy, and the fact that when they made up stories together about, for instance, their own cats, they were so united in their invention it was as if they inhabited the same brain.

Aside from the Riders' separate bedrooms, there were several details about Laura that the people of Hartley would have thought they had no need to consider. They knew she was artistic with plants, but landscape and horticulture were subjects they believed a girl could learn about by looking at seed catalogues. They did not know that she had lived with her sister for a year, and nearly every day gone to the University Library to study garden books. Also, she read novels, a habit none of her friends, and no one in the family, shared. It was a quirk her sisters would think was an affectation—Laura, the community-college dropout, trying to show off. It was because of this imagined censure on Laura's part that she was sensitive about—and, indeed, embarrassed by her hobby. No one knew that she had read every single one of the TV Book Club novels; that is to say, she read them all until the format changed, until the show featured only dead authors. Laura had stopped cold the summer the nation of viewers were to read three books by William Faulkner. She quit after thirty pages of the first for reasons she believed that anyone interested in a comprehensible story-line could understand.

In addition to her secret pleasure in reading, Laura enjoyed writing. Nothing serious or big or personal, no journal stuffed between the mattresses, no shoe box filled with smudged pages, no amazing blog that had made her famous in cyberspace. She was satisfied with a small stage, and had nearly enough bliss using her talents to take care of the correspondence for the landscape business she and Charlie owned. She prided herself on the connections she made with her customers through her e-mails and the newsletters, communications that were general and at the same time, it seemed to her, confiding. *It is to my great surprise that my delphiniums still keep coming up, year after year.* This method of relationship was far more gratifying to her than speaking by phone or in person. For one thing, she was an entirely different Laura on the screen; she liked herself far better in print. It was curious, that she was so much more interesting and witty and sure when no other human being was present, when the correspondent was nothing but an idea. She wondered what it meant, that she could only be her ultimate self when she was alone.

"Shhhhh," she'd begin like a prayer when she entertained her most private fantasy, a vision, a gauzy thing she had never mentioned to anyone. Where she used to fantasize about certain professional men and also about getting a collie, this innermost dream did not flicker, did not fade. The strength of her yearning for it had only grown as the years passed. She would lie on her bed in the spare room where she slept, and close her eyes, and she'd see herself sitting in a wing chair in a long pale skirt, and a cashmere cardigan lightly studded with moth holes. Charlie would say, if she had ever told him, that she was having a past-life experience, a life in which she did not, with utmost care, seal away her sweaters in the cedar chest. In her vision there was usually a cup of tea on the table, and a burning cigarette in a flowered china ashtray, not that she had ever really smoked. How could she describe this castle in the air to anyone? How could she explain how comforting this abiding image was to her? She saw herself being still and thinking. That was it; that was the fantasy. Although she did not know anyone who was a reader, although she'd spent her childhood watching television, and now Nick at Nite was often on until midnight in the Rider house, Laura wanted, in a dress that came to her ankles and in robin's-egg-blue high-heeled leather Mary Janes, to be an author.

The first time the dream took on real shape, the first time there was an object in her mind's eye, a material thing, pages wrapped in a rose-colored dust jacket, soft and dense as velvet, was the evening she not only met, but spoke to Jenna Faroli in the basement of the Hartley Public Library. Jenna Faroli! The host of the Milwaukee Public Radio *Jenna Faroli Show.* Jenna Faroli, the single famous person in the town of Hartley, not counting Tom Lawler, who'd been voted off after three episodes of *Survivor*; a Mrs. America contestant; and a grandmother who had raised marijuana for her grandson, a dowager who had had to serve time.

Jenna Faroli's husband, Frank Voden, was a judge on the Wisconsin Supreme Court, and though he was prominent, certainly, and important, no one would have cared about him if he hadn't had his lustrous wife. The pair had recently moved to Hartley, midway between Frank's court in Madison and the radio station in Milwaukee, in an effort to secure privacy and quiet. Hartley residents tended to be conservative, and yet Laura had noticed a bragging tone in their complaints about the judge. Charlie, in a flash of wisdom, had explained this by saying that the Faroli-Vodens, even if they were leftist fucknuts, were now Hartley's own.

Whatever people thought of Frank Voden was of little interest to Laura. Jenna Faroli, she was sure, was universally loved by her listeners. Because to listen to Jenna was to love her. There were subtle noises she made when she was speaking—nothing as vulgar as lip smacking, but rather, what sounded like the softest parting of her lips, such delicately made plosives. You could hear her smile, the creases of it; you could hear how she must be leaning toward her guest if he was in the studio; you could hear the sweet urgency of her curiosity. She was an intellectual, someone with range, someone with breadth of knowledge. One morning she might talk with Jane Goodall, and the next a potentially dull person like Alan Greenspan, and the day after, David Bowie. She was able to make even the Federal Reserve interesting, because she knew that somewhere deep within every subject was the land mine of human relations. Laura had analyzed Jenna's method and had concluded that Jenna could find the story in any topic because she understood that there was no such thing as happiness in the middle of the narrative. *Narrative*, as a matter of fact, was a word that Laura had learned from the great JF. It didn't matter if she was interviewing Sharon Stone or a half-dead senator, or a doctor specializing in cancer of the gums, or the man who had caught the largest fish in the state of Wisconsin. Jenna Faroli seemed able to see into anyone's life and so ask questions that articulated a problem the guest might not even know he had. For some time, she had not been a household name outside of Milwaukee Public Radio's fame, outside of that small circle of the brainy, but five or so years before, the show had been syndicated, and Jenna Faroli's voice now rippled out into the nation.

Laura first met her the night she took eighteen potted plants, old and new favorites, to the Hartley Garden Club. The rumor had started a week before: Jenna Faroli was going to join. Laura was going to stand before the twenty-five members, the Hartley High Society, women to whom she would forever be in service. They had asked that she explain the virtues and care of each perennial, and she also planned to show them a crafty way of cheering up a room with container gardens in galvanized-steel buckets wrapped in sticky floral shelf paper and ribbon. As Charlie had said, "They love that shit."

The Hartley ladies, with their garden club and book club, Friends of the Library, and their college-bound children, had no idea how pretty Laura Rider, through the years, had improved herself, how a decade before, for instance, she had started listening to public radio because an older woman employee, a crank, had insisted upon it in the greenhouse. When Laura listened to authors talking about their books she could actually feel her mind, the ant colony of it, the bustle and movement up there, the building of tunnels, the carrying of food. Her brain, she knew, was improving itself of its own accord.

She had never said a word to anyone about how she considered Jenna Faroli to be her teacher. Charlie, maybe, sensed her infatuation, but not, surely, the extent of it. Here was another essential part of Laura Rider that she could not speak about. No one would understand the solace and the thrill of that phantom place, 90.4 FM, made possible by a bandwidth, made possible by waves as long as a football field. From ten every morning until noon she imagined that she and Jenna were alone in a sunlit room—yes, just the two of them. Laura was at a child's desk, with the top that lifts, and the deep well inside for crayons and neatly stacked workbooks. Laura, obedient and shining. How she loved slipping into the dream, master and pupil bathed in the warmth of their mutual regard. The idea, though, that in real life she might be in the same small room with Jenna at the garden club filled her with such excitement and such dread she had to pull over twice on the way in order to steady her breathing, and once for fear she might throw up.

Under any circumstances it is surprising and sometimes disappointing, and even unnerving, to see a radio personality, particularly after feeling intimate with the voice, that voice which seems the whole of the person. Laura, unfortunately, had identified Jenna at the grocery store a month earlier and so already had had the shock. She was prepared for the disjunction, for the fact that Jenna was not, as she had imagined, a woman with an ample bosom in a cream-colored suit, a knot of blond hair at her nape, milky skin down her throat, and medium-sized pearls glowing in her ears. Jenna in the flesh was awkwardly tall, flat-chested, dark-haired, and her large wide feet, in her sensible shoes, were duckishly turned out. She was nothing like the beauty her rich, warm voice suggested. Laura had thought how unfair it was that in the twenty-first century, when so much help is available, smart women were still often not attractive, and yet, on the other hand, Jenna didn't seem to make much effort. She had looked as if she'd taken no care at all, a smudge of lipstick on her shapeless mouth, and two black lines, also smeared, under her small gray eyes. The makeup did nothing to highlight what may have been her best features. She wore silky sack clothing, the sort made for women who have given up. Laura had wondered if it was possible—could it be?—that Jenna had even the smallest inferiority complex when it came to her appearance. How strange that would be, and yet Laura's love for her would be redoubled if it were true. The more she thought about it, the more she realized how awful it would have been if Jenna were beautiful, how much more terrifying it would have been if Laura had to stand before the Jenna Faroli of her imagination, a woman who was mythically glamorous as well as knowledgeable, wise, articulate, kind, and deep.

Jenna would have occasion to remember that first meeting with Mrs. Rider. She remembered Laura's apparent sweetness, the moussey drenched look of the blond curls that framed her face, the rosy blush, and the way she'd demurely lowered her eyes and then, as if in that shy moment she'd given herself a pep talk, she'd lifted her graceful head and gazed directly at Jenna. There was the charm, too, of the library's basement, the glossy salmon-colored paint on the cement floor, the faux-wood paneling, the case of trophies suspended from the ceiling, relics from a long-ago Hartley triumph. Jenna had come to the garden club because she did not want to seem standoffish in her new community, and because she did mean to plant a bed of flowers. She had come even though she despised clubs, especially those that were sure to attract no one but women.

She sized up the group in her first glance. The members were the upper crust, the wives of doctors and lawyers from the surrounding area, or perhaps, she thought, the Hartley women were themselves professional. It was hard to tell. They had good dye jobs, the silver and golden blond streaked through the gray, and many of them wore pleated slacks and matching jackets, and flats on their feet, their arms jangling with bracelets, all of it meant to seem casual. They were standing in tight clusters, as they may well have done on the school yard in seventh grade. Jenna had learned to be careful of her own sex, and although she appreciated a woman's easy intimacy in the studio, off the air she admired restraint. Off the air she longed for reticence. In the library basement she went straight to Laura's display, to the table of virgin's bower, crested iris, lenten rose, and lungwort.

"How lovely," she murmured, bending over the blooms. She wanted a sweep of beauty in her yard, however that could be had. Often her listeners were eager to meet her, but when they did they stared, trying to put voice and face together, which, Jenna knew, was a struggle.

Laura had squatted down to get her box of brochures from under the table, and when she stood up, there, right in front of her, was her idol. In spite of her rich fantasy life, she had never imagined the first seconds, the introductory moment. "Ha!" was what came out of her mouth on a sharp inhale.

Jenna remembered first thinking that Laura Rider was trying to make the mental leap, trying to square the fact of Jenna's unruly hair, the ungainly figure, with the disembodied silky voice. Or did the woman have a fever? Her color was high, her wide blue eyes were glassy, her puffy lips parted in a small *o*. "Are you all right?" Jenna said, reaching across, touching Laura's forearm.

"Me?" Laura breathed. What she'd give for a second chance, and yet she idiotically said again, "Me?"

Jenna couldn't help admiring the style of the plant woman, a contrast to the constrained beige uniforms of the garden club members. Laura Rider was wearing a straight denim dress with a toothy shiny zipper down the front as if in mockery— or was it in homage to a farmer's coveralls? She had boldly cinched it at the waist with a wide leather belt in the muted soft purple of liver. On her the effect was somehow both elegant and humorous.

"It seems warm in here," Jenna said, "and I was only yesterday with someone who fainted. So now I suppose I'm afraid everyone I see is going to keel over, one by one, all these ladies collapsing. Imagine the sound of those bracelets at the same time hitting the floor, the point of impact."

Laura burst out laughing, her hands clapped to her mouth. She had grown up in Casey, the next town to the west, and she, the upstart from the rival high school, had dated the brothers of some of these women.

"Is that shock or glee?" Jenna asked, leaning into the table as if the better to see for herself.

Laura wasn't going to look, but she sincerely hoped that the women of Hartley were observing that, of all the people in the room, Jenna Faroli had chosen to talk to Laura Rider. "I, I played basketball at Casey High." She was speaking through her smile, through her laughter, the words bubbling from her mouth. "I was on the team, the shooting guard, my fifteen minutes of fame, and one time the sister of Cassie Johnson, she's over by the flag, tried to beat me up after a game." Shock or glee? Laura was being interviewed by Jenna Faroli! "I almost married Patty Heiderman's—she's the one in red—her brother." Mark Heiderman was the reason Laura had dropped out of community college, escaped to her sister's, hadn't shown her face in Hartley for a year. Mark Heiderman had socked her in the stomach when she'd gotten pregnant, and Patty had slain her verbally in public, at the car wash, when she'd found out Laura had had an abortion.

"I'm sure there is so much in the understory of a small town," Jenna said, "so much a stranger, no matter how long she lives here, can never know. From the outside, though, I tell you, it all looks wonderfully serene. It seems to us like heaven." She picked up one of Laura's brochures. "So—you're not going to faint even if you secretly wish everyone here would, and you sell perennials, and you do landscaping. Prairie Wind Farm."

"Yes, yes, we do. My husband, my husband, Charlie, Charlie Rider, and I have had the business for—oh my gosh—over ten years."

Jenna would remember that, too, the first time she heard his name. "Charlie Rider," she mused. She knew that she shouldn't bring up the title of a book to this woman, and yet, even as she meant to stop herself, the sentence was floating between them: "Have you ever read *Brideshead Revisited*?" Why was she asking? Why did she persist in referring to books when it was obvious the listener would not have read them. "Or seen the miniseries?" Jenna added with little optimism.

Although Laura nodded with great enthusiasm, although she grinned hard, she was sure Jenna would be able to tell that she had never heard of it.

"I say so," Jenna forged on, "because Charles Ryder is the name of the narrator, a blank slate of a young man, very impressionable, who goes up to Oxford. To study there, that is. He becomes captivated—obsessed, really—by nearly everyone in a wealthy Catholic family. He falls in love with the idea of them. He loves them and observes them and chronicles their downfall."

"My Charlie," Laura exclaimed, "would do something like that!"

Jenna thrust her nose into the blooms again and said, "How lucky you are to raise such exquisite things." She had recently decided that, in the balance and in general, she hated people, but in spite of this new self-knowledge, she couldn't help finding the individual person interesting and often heartbreaking.

"This is our love, Charlie's and mine. Our real love is the nursery."

"How lucky," Jenna repeated. Why had she mentioned *Brideshead*? She sometimes disliked herself more than she disliked the population at large. Why lecture this stranger about one of her favorite novels, a wonderfully sentimental book about decline, the sorrow of aging, the loss of love, the end of a glorious era for the landed gentry? It was funny, of course it was, the way Laura had so happily said, "My Charlie would do something like that," without having any idea that the fictional Charles Ryder was actually a colorless, depressed character. Still, how could the name Charlie Rider come up without Jenna's mentioning *Brideshead*?

In an effort to redeem herself, she began to talk. "I'm a beginner," she said, "and so I feel as if I'm here under false pretenses. I don't have time right now to be a regular member of the club, or go through the Master Gardener course, but I'm dying to make a garden, to do the actual work, to plant—to get back, somehow, to . . ." She hardly knew what she was trying to explain, an unusual predicament for her. "I want to be outside and have my hands in the dirt, a primal sort of desire, I guess. The idea that a person can make something as fantastic as the pictures in the books I've looked at seems preposterous, all that beauty of your own making. With this garden business I feel naïve and ignorant and arrogant, too.

As if I think I could become a brain surgeon by reading a manual, or a best-selling novelist because I like books."

"Not at all!" Laura cried. From the corner of her eye she could see that Patty Heiderman had rotated 180 degrees to stare in her direction. "We can work out a color palette in relation to the shade and the sun in your yard." Imagine Jenna Faroli at the farm, sitting in the wicker chair in the shed with Laura, the books spread out on the table, the color wheel before them. It was a reversal of the fantasy: Laura, the teacher; Jenna, the student. She was not as ugly as Laura remembered, or maybe she seemed somewhat attractive—*handsome* was perhaps the word—because she was speaking. Laura could now fully understand why the radio guests revealed themselves to Jenna in the interviews. In person and in a large room, it was just as if Laura were alone in her car with Jenna on the radio, with that voice, the color of it a warm buttery yellow. "There are many hardy varieties," Laura went on, reaching over to touch Jenna's arm, the same gesture Jenna had made a few minutes earlier. If it was Patty Heiderman's gaze that spurred her to this intimacy, so what? "I could guide you, if you came to the farm, if that seemed like a good idea to you. You can learn as you go and at the same time have fun. You can have real pleasure with the basics."

"Pleasure with the basics," Jenna murmured.

"I sometimes tell my customers, I say, What did God know about horticulture when He created the Garden? He probably made it with dumb luck, and there were probably plants Eve later dug up and moved around. But even God at a certain point just had to plunge in."

Laura was always honest up to a point, careful to explain that the learning curve could be expensive if you didn't have a watering schedule and if you didn't fertilize your investment. If you had lousy taste—a problem afflicting many of her customers—then you would be blissfully ignorant of the atrocity out back, the mismatched colors and the inevitable silly impatiens thrown in to cover the dying perennials that Laura had painstakingly advised. It was hard to say who were worse, the haughty, demanding Illinois vacationers, or the relaxed Wisconsin women in their oversized appliquéd shirts, bursting out of their Capri pants. Laura wanted to say to Jenna how impossible it was to remain a nice person if you so much as had eyes in your head; Laura was not nearly as kind, she knew, or as generous, as Jenna Faroli.

If she'd been truthful with Jenna, she would have said she was ready to sell the business, chuck the farm, get out while they were having success. Keeping the place watered and weeded and mowed, managing the employees, coming up with workshops, designing new beds, tearing out the old, dealing with the customers whose peonies weren't the right color—she had had enough. She would have explained to Jenna that the huge sellers at Prairie Wind, the steel buckets wrapped in shelf paper, planted with geraniums and sweet woodruff, were a rip-off at fifty dollars, and she was embarrassed, too, even though they were high-end, by the terracotta angels and frogs and owls, the grapevine wreaths, the wind chimes, the plaster birdbaths. The thought of another season made her want to vanish all of a sudden, to drive off, no note left behind. She could breed dogs, maybe, in a new life, in Nova Scotia or British Columbia. She looked into the gray eyes of Jenna Faroli and she silently asked this question: What, Jenna, is my calling? What is my true love?

Laura wanted to tell Jenna how she had worked to improve herself, in spite of quitting William Faulkner. She had, for a time, read the titles in the Hartley Library's book club. She hadn't ever gone to the evening meetings, but she had tried to be loyal to the member that was herself. It wasn't always easy, because in her opinion some of the books were wordy, dull, interminable. Hello! We don't have all day here! She often couldn't help thinking that if the hero and heroine had only been able to get ahold of medication there would not have been any occasion for a story. Holden Caulfield would have been fine on Prozac, and ditto for the Professor in his dusty old house, in the dreary Willa Cather novel that she had not been able to finish.

While Jenna was asking her questions about potting soil and pruning, and while Laura was answering in detail, she was imagining that she was telling Jenna the essential facts of her life. She was saying what she'd never say to anyone else; she was saying, "I think, Jenna, I think I want to write a book." She was sure, if she said so, that Jenna would spur her on, just as Laura was cheering her on about gardening.

It occurred to her, in the middle of the discussion of Jenna's ailing hydrangea, the six in her front yard, that what Laura most wanted to write was a novel about a plain woman who becomes beautiful. A story that finally discovers what a woman needs and wants, and there in the distance is the man who can meet those requirements, the man coming closer and closer to her, the woman's beauty snapping into focus as he arrives. She shivered even as she was speaking to Jenna about the wonder of mushroom compost. Although Laura Rider was finished with sex, she was not the least bit tired of romance. She looked into the small but knowing and sympathetic eyes of Jenna Faroli, and she said to herself, I want to write a book about love.

# Chapter 2

A FEW WEEKS AFTER THE GARDEN-CLUB MEETING, CHAR-
lie Rider and Jenna Faroli met along Highway S outside of
Hartley. This encounter occurred by chance. "Or," Charlie
later said, "did it?" The month was May, the wheat and al-
falfa were waving in the soft breeze, the green was so bright
in the sunlight, making the pastures and fields so shiny, it all
looked like a plastic backdrop. Wasn't it as if, Charlie would
ask her, the Silver People, on an avenue named S, had called
to them on that spring day of the spangly colors, when nature
looked more phony than phony nature? The Silver People,
the glowing dwarfs who inhabited Charlie's private universe.
He happened to be driving in front of Jenna, and it was he
who pulled over on the wide gravel shoulder to look across
the field to the horizon.

Nature in general was such a dazzling, goofball thing,

always bubbling up out of nowhere, always morphing into a crazy something else; one minute you've about killed yourself digging out all the thistles in the field, and the next, garlic mustard has spread itself right behind your back. Son of a bitch—nature! And what a sense of humor, blowing your house down, say, and what do you find under the mud floor of the basement but a fossilized T. rex? Thank you very much. The next minute, the trickster goes into ravishing mode without any effort: mist on a pond, the crescent moon—So don't look at me!—the whole place lit up in blossom time for no one but the bees. What was behind it all, beyond it, not to mention right in front of us? Who knew how many dimensions, scrim after scrim, a person could peel back into if he took the time to pay attention? "Don't start," his wife often said to him when he was gearing up on this subject. "What you see is what you get. Reality is reality, period."

Would Jenna have stopped on Highway S if he hadn't led the way? She wondered if she would have ignored the bobbing lights in her eagerness to get home if he hadn't, by pulling over, guided her toward awe. "What are they?" she called to him as she climbed out of the car. She had her hand to her brow, looking, not at the stranger next to her, but at the six or so quivering spheres past the silos, the barns, just above the tree line. "Are we having floaters?" she said. "Both of us? Do we need to see an ophthalmologist right now? Or a shrink?"

Ah, that voice. He was having an out-of-body experience hearing it in the flesh. He had known it was Jenna Faroli who would step from the car, because he'd been watching her from his rearview mirror for the two miles she'd been behind him. He didn't listen to her program, but whenever he heard it in the background he wished she would stop talking. He wanted her to sing along with him in the sound track that was often going in his head, principally the old-time string-band music he'd learned from his grandfather. "Short Life of Trouble," "June Apple," "Going Across the Mountain." She must have a pure and yet sweetly lusty singing voice, with a spine-tingling vibrato. For a minute he forgot the spheres. The Grand Ole Opry: he's up there with Jenna, and here comes Dolly, boobs like traffic cones, and, wait, Emmylou, she's belting out "Pretty Little Girl" with them, too.

"Or do we need a neurosurgeon," Jenna was saying, "are our brain tumors flaring up?"

Charlie closed his eyes, took a deep breath, raised his full glass to life. Jenna Faroli—biggest cranium on the planet, according to his wife—and here he was with her, looking out to the world revealed. "There's nothing wrong with your vision," he said, blinking, checking his own. "Or your circuitry, I suspect, nope, not a thing. You probably don't have psychiatric troubles, either. Clean bill of health. They, those lights—they might be what you think they are."

It was then that she turned to look at him. Out of long habit, she masked her censure in the singsong of her satiny tones. "And what do I think they are?"

It wasn't the tender shape of his dark eyes or his unlashed

smile, ear to ear, that first drew her attention, or even his corkscrew curls, the tight spring of them, but the pleading in the long, tapered fingers with the flat pads, as he held them out, in prayer position.

"Here's my guess," he said. "You don't really think those lights are UFOs, and you could never say that they might be, you wouldn't really even consider it, because then everyone within range of 90.4 FM would think you'd flipped. *UFOs* aren't even the word you want for what's out there. You're thinking spirit world. You're thinking alternative reality, maybe. You've heard about ionic disturbances, so you could go the science route. But this seems like something different from that description. It's possible you'd like them to be magical. It's possible you want to be charmed."

She said nothing. She used what her producer in the studio called Jenna's I-hate-you smile, the tilted head, the closed mouth spread to 45-percent capacity, the sincere nod. She had recently done a show about Yeats's beliefs in palmistry, astral travel, and crystal gazing, about the poet's falling under the spell of the mystic Helena Petrovna Blavatsky. Her guest had gone on to the question in general of well-educated and discriminating people who give themselves over to the occult. Jenna did not doubt that the sacrifice of Yeats's reason, the force of his sheer wackiness, had yielded great benefits to the culture at large. But in the moment she had never wanted less to be charmed by alternative reality. The one miracle she believed in was kindness—but only if it wasn't talked about.

She was of course open to all points of view, even those of a presumptuous kook. Her stranger's jeans were so crisp she wondered if they'd been starched and ironed, and the sleeves of his light-green shirt had been neatly rolled up, each to the same level on his forearm. Even as Jenna considered the spectacle at the edge of the sky, she noted that Charlie looked like a schoolboy whose mother had dressed him.

"Are they benign?" she asked. "Those beings caravanning in the spheres?"

"Would you like them to be?"

She again turned to her companion. "I'd like them to be as well dressed as you."

He nodded thoughtfully. "It's hard, though, to look like this when you're traveling. When you've come from so far."

"Yes, that's true. Especially because you would have had to start out—let's see—a million miles per hour, and if you came from the nearest star, that's Alpha Centauri, so . . . wouldn't you have had to start out at roughly . . . give me a minute . . . I'm not quite sure about the math, but something like the time of Moses?"

"Whoa!" he said. "Math! Wow." His whole body now seemed to be nodding, the bounce coming from his heels. "But maybe, maybe you have to do that thing where you shift the—what's it called?—the paradigm. Isn't it possible that they have other ways to travel? Maybe our laws have nothing to do with theirs. Maybe they can surf the astral plane, or even travel on our thoughts."

"Poor things! My thoughts would certainly rumple their clothing. Still, however they get here, I maintain that it's important to make a good impression."

"You don't like the green bodysuit? Too casual? You wish they'd snazz it up a little, make an effort? Accessorize?"

"I have large feet, so I always think if you're a dainty size you should use that. You should wear elegant shoes, at the least." In her brown oxfords she stepped closer to the field. "What else do I want in my aliens?" She squinted hard at the sky. "Let me just say I refuse to be frightened of creatures smaller than me and those whose pallor is green. I'd like to think they were getting a charge out of us, out of our dramas, that we were providing them with a degree of entertainment. That is, I hope we're not too dull. Not that I want to be made fun of, no, but I'd like them to be lovingly amused. I'd like them to feel as if they'd seen a masterpiece—a Preston Sturges film, for instance. I'd like them to feel as if the world, our world, was a generous place. A tall order, to be sure." She smiled at him, a genuine smile this time. "I'd like them to feel lighthearted."

He was staring at her, all movement suspended. "I don't know you," he said after a minute. "I mean, I know you—you know I know you, but I don't know you. If you know what I mean. So it doesn't make sense for me to want to tell you a secret. But—I'd like to. I'd like to tell you one."

"You probably shouldn't," she said, "since you don't know me."

He noodled the gravel with the toe of his boot. "I can appreciate that—but if you have any questions, about what you're seeing? Not that I'm an expert . . ." He rooted around in his pocket and pulled out a card for her. "If you find yourself thinking about this scene, you could e-mail me, and I'll tell you what I know."

"Charlie Rider," Jenna said. She was not going to bring up the Charles Ryder of *Brideshead Revisited*. "I met your wife a few weeks ago at the library. She was very helpful."

"The indomitable Mrs. Rider," Charlie sang out. "It was the greatest night of her life, talking to you."

"I doubt that," Jenna said. "At least, I hope it's not true. Please do thank her again for me. And thank you for this—"

"Miracle."

"Card," she said firmly. "Thanks for the card." The restrained, tasteful font was Eaglefeather, the invention of Frank Lloyd Wright. You could tell a person's class, or his aspirations anyway, his pretensions, perhaps, by his font. Someone else, she was sure, had designed the card for him. If you had such a lavish head of hair and an impish face, if you had excitement pulsing in your eyes, you wouldn't be able to see clear to a font like Eaglefeather. As she got in the car, she called back to him, "But what the hell are they?"

"If I told you," he said, walking toward her, coming alongside her Toyota, "if I told you about the Silver People, you wouldn't believe me."

"It all depends on how you tell it."

"I don't even believe me when I tell myself the story."

"Then you'd better get to work on your narrative skills."

"Narrative skills," he echoed. He stuck his hand through her open window. "Charlie Rider," he said, shaking what he had grasped, shaking her fingertips. "It's an honor to meet you. A real thrill."

Charlie had always had confidence. He was the sixth and final child in his family. His mother had understood by baby number three that there was little point in worrying, and by baby number five, no point in trying to mold. By the time he came, her wisdom was honed to a comfortable dull edge, that line she worked between concern and neglect. As an infant, Charlie had been happy to lie on his back nibbling his toes, singing to himself, and watching his grandfather play his fiddle. His mother loved his shining eyes, his astonishing curls, and the dreaminess that would later make his teachers want to smack him. The other children had straight hair, were good in math, and had chubby legs. Where had Charlie come from? Once he could crawl, he had the habit of throwing himself into the family swimming pool, and for years he believed the story his brother told him, that he was a creature who had been born of a fish. He believed, that is, that his own real mother was capable of transformation. No fish-child has ever been so variously and well dressed, from matador, to pirate, to magician, to king, to nurse—all professions that required capes and millinery. He drank a bottle until he was seven, pouring the milk from the refrigerator into the Evenflo, and screwing on the blue-rimmed nipple that had a chewed hole the size of his thumb. When his older brothers beat him up at home they were mild about it, and out in the world they defended him. He was lucky in their protection. He seemed, though, not to care much about what anyone thought of him. And he didn't ever consider himself to be in danger. It was his native happiness, that radiant, dreamy joy, that both invited teasing and shielded him from it.

When he was seventeen and flunking out of high school, a twenty-five-year-old woman named Shirley lured him away from the pool table at Nybo's Tavern, drove him to her uncle's house on Lake Margaret, and taught him in one night so many things he wondered if he should make a list of the pleasures in order not to forget. He recalled the way she had drawn his lower lip into her own mouth, the way she had licked his pants before she'd removed them, and the pressure of her finger in a place he had not before considered would hold any interest to a second party. He realized, as he tried to imagine what he would write, that Shirley's teachings were not things a boy could scribble in a notebook. What had happened with Shirley was a wordless miracle, just as music was, a dissolving happiness into the cosmos. It was essential, then, to keep singing, to keep making love, to keep creating the songs note by note as the sound, note by note, vanished.

After graduation, made possible by Principal Stapleton's generous interpretation of his efforts, Charlie found jobs here and there around Hartley. He met Laura; they often had sex three times a day; they dabbled in horticulture, including growing marijuana; they bought the farm with money Charlie inherited from his grandfather; they started the business; and they got married. By the time he was forty, he felt that the adventure was over. His wife was never going to sleep with him again; hundreds of people traipsed around their property through the spring and summer, and he would work to keep it at that trembling point of perfection, as per Mrs. Rider's orders; he would sing "Eyes like Cherries" and other Grandpa Rider songs at the annual St. Lucy's School fund-raiser; he would marvel at the universe, trying to see into it—and that was his lot. He understood that his feelings of decline were ancient ones, that men before him had suffered in the same way. He knew this because he had been exposed to some classics on the stage—two Shakespeare, one Chekhov. In high school, Mrs. Garstucky had taken them to see *Uncle Vanya* in Chicago, and he remembered a scene where Vanya, played by George C. Scott, had said something like "I'm forty-seven. How am I going to get through the next years of my life? What shall I do? How shall I fill up these years?" Charlie had come home from the play, and, standing on the lip of the swimming pool fully clothed, he had given his mother that speech in Scott's growly voice, and then fallen over into the water. There was no one who laughed as hard at him as his mother. Now, at forty-five, he understood Vanya's sentiments; he could see they were no joke.

It wasn't that life was unhappy or that difficult, not at all. He was married to his Captain of Industry. They owned their farm, and their business was more successful than they'd imagined it could be at the start. With sixteen employees, he had become, to the surprise of his siblings, a boss. This had never been his goal, in part because he'd never had any particular goals. He loved to sing his grandfather's songs. He liked to pluck at the banjo. He enjoyed drawing. He loved thinking about what lay beyond the blue sky. He'd loved lying on the floor channeling himself into the dream life of their dog, Beaver; he'd imagine Beaver chasing a squirrel, and by and by the real-life mutt would start twitching and whining in his sleep. There were no limits to the powers of the mind, no limit to what was out in that swirl of gas and infinity. A person, however, did not get paid to inhabit the dream life of a dog or love the mysteries of this world, and so it was best that he and Laura had Prairie Wind Farm Inc. It was probably better than doing hospital transport, although he had enjoyed that job, wheeling patients from surgery to recovery and then to their rooms. He had met Laura en route to having her appendix removed.

It was Laura who had grown the business, Laura who every day gave all of them their marching orders, saving for her husband the jobs that she was pretty sure he could pull off without ruining the machinery or plowing up a section of orchids, or planting the row of twenty-five peonies in the wrong yard. It was Laura, his family believed, who had saved Charlie, who had made the nutcase—the adorable, the lovable nutcase, to be sure—into a solid citizen and a happy man.

# Chapter 3

ON THE WAY HOME, JENNA FOUND HERSELF MORE INTER-
ested in the idea of Charlie Rider than in the celestial spheres,
the ionic disturbances, the travelers from Coma Berenices—
whatever they were. The lights, she was sure, could be explained, and so, presumably, could Charlie Rider, and yet in
the moment he seemed the greater mystery. He had wanted
to tell her something, and he'd been both persistent and patient, both cocksure and pleasantly uncertain. He'd been earnest and whimsical, two qualities that do not always go hand
in hand. She had not wanted to hear about his experience
with the UFOs while she'd been with him, but the farther she
was from him, the more curious she grew. It seemed to her
good fortune to have watched the aliens with someone who
could have passed for one himself, an alien who didn't take
his species too seriously.

Jenna had always been privately scornful of people who dabbled in the occult. As a child, she had not been able to get spooked by playing Mary Worth in front of a mirror or contacting the dead via the Ouija board. At the age of nine, she had understood that what bored girls do is try to scare themselves silly. She was willing to grant that victims of alien abduction had complex disorders, or at the least a vague cultural malaise, and shouldn't be dismissed, but she couldn't work up much sympathy for the type. She wondered if at the root of their troubles wasn't the childish need to have a frightening element in their lives. She wondered what Mrs. Rider—the feverish, stylish, *indomitable* Mrs. Rider—thought about Charlie's interest in the supernatural. She wondered if a woman who looked so mild could be more or less invincible. Did the Riders listen to the *Jenna Faroli Show* while they worked side by side in the greenhouse potting geraniums? She liked that idea, Mr. and Mrs. Rider, a part of her life without her knowing it, without her ever having to know.

At dinner, over veal birds, *oiseaux sans têtes,* Jenna described the lights to her husband. "They were blurry and bobbing," she said. "It was so strange I pulled over to get a better look."

"Weather balloons, no doubt," Frank said, his nose to the cunning slices of veal he'd wrapped around a filling of mushrooms and butter and basil. He'd been a Rhodes scholar, and therefore as he sliced down through his ribboned creation he held his utensils in the continental style. There had been nothing more miraculous in Jenna's life than Frank's recent verve in the kitchen. He had taken charge when they'd remodeled the 1868 fieldstone farmhouse, insisting on eight burners, three sinks, two ovens, granite countertops, the overhead rack for the new pots and pans, and a pantry to store the gadgets. "Or they were earth tremors," he said, "which cause electromagnetic fields. The intensity of the fields, of the luminosities, can be stunning. They can cause alterations in TV and radio reception, power outages—they can knock people insensible."

"I could almost imagine," she said, "if you were prone to that kind of thing, thinking that those lights were UFOs. They seemed to have an intelligence, bobbing and dancing in relation to each other."

"The revolt of the soul," he pronounced, "against the intellect. Goodbye, Jenna Faroli. In case you were thinking to retrieve an abduction memory, they are formed, you know, just as beliefs in witches, incubi, and Satan are. The United States leads in UFO reporting, because we have more practicing hypnotists than any other country in the world. But when there's a real physical phenomenon, when there are luminosities which, as I said, have been known to give people tingling sensations and actual paralysis—why not"—he took a bite and chewed for a moment, his eyes shut—"call it the work of aliens? Do you think there's too much paprika?"

"I'm weeping, Frankie. Can't you see? I'm weeping because this is the most delicious thing I've ever eaten."

"It's somewhat overboard on the paprika." He drew a small leather book out of his apron pocket and wrote himself a note, tucked it back in the pocket, and returned his attention to his plate and his subject. "Whitley Strieber's books have probably done more to standardize the alien experience for victims than possibly even Hollywood movies—"

"But you can understand the impulse to believe," she said, her voice raised only slightly, "especially in people who have religious longings, people who are disaffected from their church. Maybe they can't get interested in science. Maybe they want to do something contrarian or rebellious." She could all at once imagine that Charlie Rider, a lifelong Hartley resident, had found his way to be an individual by having an experience with an extraterrestrial. She leaned over her place setting toward her husband. "And it's not drag racing or drug addiction or gang mayhem. It's harmless."

"Harmless? Most abductees, a huge percentage, say that their encounters with UFOs have had a devastating effect on their lives." With his mouth full he said, "And it's not far-fetched to say that occultism has on occasion gone hand in hand with reactionary ideologies." He swallowed, swiping his mouth with his napkin. "Maybe it's harmless here, in our somewhat stable democracy. But you could make a connection without that much trouble, connecting, for example, Theosophy with Nazi ideology."

"Uh-huh," she said. She didn't think that Charlie Rider had had a frightening encounter with his Silver People—as he'd called them—or that he'd turn his beliefs toward fascism. He was in the minority, surely, one of those who had tripped the light fantastic with the space travelers, who had had a jolly night out. "One could argue," she pressed on, "that perfectly ordinary people need to detach religious impulses from any entrenched creed, and so they fall into the refreshment of the occult. But I'll settle for the globes' being weather balloons, even though I think I'm disappointed."

There were several reasons Frank knew everything. In the course of a thirty-year career in the law, eight as public defender, four as district attorney, and finally holding forth from various benches, including now the bench of the state supreme court, he had seen cases that touched on a great many subjects. His capacious mind was superbly organized, and so there was very little he forgot, very little in the archive he could not access. But the real cause of his erudition, Jenna often said, was his abuse of literature. His addiction was a joke in the family—Frank the user, the biblioholic—and it was also something of a problem. He read, his wife thought, pathologically. It was fine to read the Russian novels again and again, fine to read criticism, the belletristic essay, military history, science, biography, collections of letters, and the occasional grocery-store mystery. It was not fine that early in the marriage they had had strife when Jenna banned him from reading at dinner, that she had to prohibit him from turning on the light immediately following sexual intercourse—as if for everyone postcoital entertainment always included V. S. Pritchett—and that she had once caught him in the shower, one hand thrust from the curtain, reading her father's inscribed first-edition copy of Bertrand Russell's *History of Western Philosophy*. She liked to tell her friends, and on occasion her radio audience, how frightened Frank became if there wasn't printed matter near his person. Their car had once broken down, and for some unexplained—perhaps paranormal—reason, they'd had no reading material for the two hours they'd had to wait for rescue. Frank had almost gone mad. There had not even been the Saab manual. He sweated and he paced, reciting all the soliloquies that were his set pieces, roving through *Othello*, *Lear*, *Merchant*, *Midsummer Night's Dream*, *As You Like It*, *Hamlet*, and a few sonnets as well. He had, however, learned to cope without a book over the sacred dinner hour, and in fact, when he had made a dazzling effort, driving to upscale markets to buy Chilean sea bass and cranking out pasta by hand, he was happy to linger at the table with his port and his wife.

If Jenna had to choose between the asset of Frank's erudition and his pleasure in the new kitchen, she would be tempted, even though she relied on his intellect for her work, to tip toward Chef Voden. Many nights a week she walked in the door to find him in a blue-and-pink-striped denim apron pulled tight around his stout middle, his glasses fogged from steam or exertion, the two or three damp hairs on his pate flattened against his shiny scalp. The chops were simmering in their glaze, the rolls baking in the oven, the sliced Ida Red apples bubbling in their cider reduction, the wine taking one heavenly breath after another. Their daughter was grown, Frank was in the kitchen, and for as long it lasted, she, Jenna Faroli, was blessed among women. The beauty of his industry! Once summer was full-blown, he would begin working on his book about jurisprudence, a tome that would run, if his other books were any indication, to fifteen hundred pages. She would enjoy his gastronomic feats, his culinary acrobatics, while she could.

The night of the bouncing globes, Frank had gone on from the subject of aliens to tell her about a fistfight that had occurred between two men in Athens, Ohio. Jenna had a fair amount of work to do and was feigning interest as best she could. One fellow in Athens believed that the Earl of Oxford had written the Shakespeare plays, whereas the other, a Stratfordian, was defending the honor of the Bard.

"Uh-huh," Jenna said again.

The trouble had begun in a chat room and escalated to the street, the two men, coincidentally in the same town, the two men, Frank said, surely yelling in iambic pentameter, while trying to puff up their puny chests. He flung his knife from side to side, crying,

"Pale trembling coward, there I throw my gage,
Disclaiming here the kindred of the king,
And lay aside my high blood's royalty. . . ."

Jenna pushed back in her chair. In the morning, she reminded Frank, she had two authors, a British woman who trained dogs, and a memoirist who had acquired four springer spaniels after he had been in an accident that damaged his frontal lobes. Those two would fill the first half of the program, and for the second a neurosurgeon from Johns Hopkins would speak about therapies for the impaired, and, finally, the actress Teri Garr would be in the studio to discuss her struggle with MS and her crusade to help those who suffered from the disease. The shows were often patchworks, including segments that invited callers, and others that were pretaped and edited. Tomorrow's program was live throughout, but in any case Jenna always liked to be overprepared.

"You should invite the Shakespeare thugs in," Frank was saying. "You'd get a tremendous number of callers, and there would be the threat of real violence to keep everyone on the edge of their car seats." He was off again:

" 'Tis not the trial of a woman's war,
   The bitter clamour of two eager tongues,
   Can arbitrate this cause betwixt us twain.
   The blood is hot . . ."

The Honorable Judge Voden leaned back and, dabbing his white linen napkin to his mouth, he giggled.

"I'll keep it in mind," Jenna said. With a glass of port in hand, she walked around the table to his chair and bent to kiss his head. "Thank you, Frankest, for the remarkable grub."

She did her best to read as much of her guests' books as she could, but she had also, through the years, become adept at scanning the pages for the heart of the matter, and zooming in on paragraphs that her producers had highlighted, those that offered up suitable questions. Jenna's standard line, when asked about her preparation, was that the author had put his time and talent and energy into his work and she would respect that labor by reading thoughtfully. It was said that she was thorough, fearless, and polite. This pleased her, and she hoped it was true. Her goal, always, was to find something to like in her guest no matter how distasteful his opinions, no matter if his book turned out to have wasted the nation's resources. She tried not to care what a guest thought of her. The pact between them was obvious and implicit. She, by virtue of her interest in him, would ask questions that would showcase his expertise or his nobility or his wit. She would try to delve without being intrusive, in the hope that he would arrive at the truth of his experience, and he would honor her by being as lively and as fascinating as he knew how. There was no predicting how it all might go, how, for instance, the minute the ON AIR sign flashed, a formerly talkative person might clam up, or a quiet one begin to jabber. Her job was to shape the interview, to keep the guest on track when necessary, to give the piece a flow when it was live so there was something of a narrative arc, and to manage the callers so that, without permitting them to rattle on, they felt heard.

When she was upstairs in the office thinking about how to approach the brain-injured patient with his spaniels, Charlie Rider came to mind again. *"If I told you about the Silver People, you wouldn't believe me."* What had she said to him? *"You'd better get to work on your narrative skills."* At dinner, Frank had said that in some quarters abduction stories were judged not by the verisimilitude of the details, but by the sincerity and emotional distress of the teller. Jenna couldn't help wondering if Charlie was a capable raconteur. She wondered what he'd have to do to make her believe, if his own doubt would make the story more convincing, if confidence would work against him. Maybe Charlie had come through the riptides of her thoughts, bobbing between the cranial waves, bursting free, and washing up on Highway S. He was silver within, the shine glowing from his astral core. Astral core? She liked the sound of it, and she pictured what such a thing might be: the deep, clear wishing well of the soul.

As she often did, she told herself that it had been a good move to come to Hartley, to leave the suburbs for this small farm surrounded by woods. She had grown tired of the women in particular in Fox Grove, tired of their fierce political correctness, the calcification of their righteousness, the competitive spirit of kitchen remodeling. She had once discovered a neighbor boy, a seven-year-old, sobbing in her scrubby bushes because on the occasion of his birthday his guests had been told to donate to their favorite cause rather than bring presents to the party. A donation to Greenpeace rather than a video game? What was wrong with the parents?

Jenna had come to the point in her forty-six years when she would rather talk with a doe-eyed elf, someone with an astral core, than have to speak over the fence to Janey Slauson about full-spectrum compact fluorescent lightbulbs. Frank and Jenna's only child, Vanessa, had made the best of a good school system in Fox Grove, and finally, after college, when the girl had gone off to get her doctorate, they'd moved fifty miles from the city. They had bought small energy-efficient cars not only because they believed in them, but to assuage their guilt about the commute, and to mitigate, as much as possible, the criticism of people like Janey Slauson.

Jenna remembered Charlie saying to her about the bouncing globes, "They might be what you think they are." Such an insolent alien! It would be difficult to do a measured show about UFOs, difficult to strike the right tone. She wouldn't want it to turn into a free-for-all, the crazies jamming the phone lines with their testimonials, but she wouldn't want them to be crushed, either, by the common sense and science of a psychologist and meteorologist. She'd done what she'd thought had been a respectful show about the community of Lily Dale, a place the spirits were said to favor. The show had been funny, in large part because the mediums she'd interviewed had had a sense of humor about their calling.

Charlie Rider had wanted to tell her a secret involving the Silver People. He was out of his radiant head, but why turn down a secret? Months away, she would ask herself what exactly propelled her to write him the first e-mail. The memoir about the spaniels and the frontal-lobe injury was, if nothing else, a testament to the human spirit, but lately Jenna was having trouble working up enthusiasm for that type of grit and endurance and good cheer; humans, she sometimes thought, had too much spirit. One of her producers, Suzie Raditz, liked to yoke together disparate subjects—in this case dogs and brains—but perhaps Suzie was having a dry spell. Perhaps Suzie needed a vacation.

Out the long windows of Jenna's study, out in the darkness, there was not a light from human or sprite or alien. There were only the sounds of the tree frogs, their strange, mournful Gregorian tones. She loved her room, the high ceiling, the curlicues in the original molding, the built-in shelves, and the comfort of her books, which had been alphabetized in the move, Achebe to Zuravleff. In her aloneness there was the draw of that most private-seeming space, the small, bright, beckoning rectangle of a blank e-mail page. It was a page that would yield company, that would people her own little world. She wondered what Charlie was telling Mrs. Rider over their dinner, wondered what they usually talked about. She would write to him because she wasn't severe and aloof, but someone who was interested in a small town personality, a woman who was investing in her new community.

It crossed her mind that by writing to him she was thumbing her nose at the likes of Janey Slauson and also Suzie Raditz. It was possible, too, that she was escaping, for just a moment, from Shakespeare; she was electronically fleeing from her husband's dishwashing down the stairs, from the noise of his recitation of *Richard II*.

# Chapter 4

THERE WERE RULES ABOUT WRITING ROMANCE NOVELS, Laura discovered. Directly after the garden-club meeting, she had gone upstairs to the stacks in the library, and checked out four how-to books. Because the rules were strict, at first the enterprise didn't sound that hard to her. If, say, your book was a Christian romance, there was to be no alcohol consumption, no magic, and the heroine and hero could not, under any circumstances, remain overnight together alone. The confusing thing was all the categories in addition to Christian: there was historical romance, futuristic, time-travel, paranormal, contemporary-comedy, chick-lit, suspense, and African American. Also gay and lesbian. What Laura wished to accomplish was more . . . *global*, maybe, was the word. She wanted to tell a story that would appeal to any woman, Every Woman. She understood that you were supposed to come up

45

with archetypes such as Wild Woman, or Earth Mother, or Passionate Artist. She thought she could do that. Everyone was, after all, something.

There had to be an intriguing plot and an emotionally intense core conflict, and then what was called the Black Moment, when there seems to be no solution for the couple in love. The Black Moment had to be one of real terror—emotional terror, that is. The manual said that creativity played a huge role. Well, obviously. If she took an honest look at herself, she would say that, on a scale from one to ten in the creativity department, she was about a seven and a half. She was creative enough to give life sparkly moments, talented enough to make pretty, theme-based tables for her nieces' birthday parties, but that sort of care and invention of course wasn't what the manual meant. She was capable of vision, certainly; the gardens and the farm itself were testaments to her taste, and her dream life, and her ability to work past the point of exhaustion. But pulling a tale of two lovers out of thin air was altogether different—not that she and Charlie didn't make up stories every day, about all kinds of things, including their four cats. The beasts had jobs and family concerns. They had supportive and troubled relationships. Their Maine coon cat, Polly, who had just gotten a new job as a bagger at the grocery store, was still in high school. In fact, big excitement: Polly was going to the prom this year. So perhaps the collaboration with Charlie was proof that Laura was not a complete beginner.

The manual that was most useful to her suggested that in order to get to know your character you could write a journal from her point of view, or have a friend pose as a reporter and interview you as your heroine. The journal was definitely the route Laura would take, after she'd determined what archetype her woman would be. She remembered a Jenna Faroli program with an author who had written a book about why women read romances, and she made a note to look it up in the online archive. As for the hero, he who provided safe harbor, she had considered for some time, long before she knew she wanted to write, what traits the perfect man should possess. It had been a purely academic question, a subject that had occupied her in the potting shed, in dinner conversations at the holidays, and through the nights when she could not sleep. Her sisters believed that women wanted to rule, but since Laura had that arrangement in her household she now and again thought it might be nice to be dominated, to live with a know-it-all who gave orders, took care of every detail, a man who was never, ha-ha, wrong. Either way, though, what most women wanted was a man who understood the rigors and rules of unconditional love. Wasn't that it? A shower of affection at the right moment, continuous and sincere reassurance, a reasonable amount of interest, and above all a well-tuned sense of timing: knowing precisely when to back off. Most adults seemed incapable of such a thing toward people who weren't their children. She wasn't even sure most parents, if called upon to demonstrate it, wouldn't have already used up their hard-worn store of love by the time their children were teenagers. That was one of the main reasons she was glad she hadn't had a baby: she wasn't convinced she would have been equal to the task.

She was pretty sure Charlie loved her as unconditionally as was humanly possible even though she had deprived him of the activity he most enjoyed. It was a terrible thing to have done to him, but the thought of returning to their old routine— No! She couldn't bear the thought of any of it, the rattling of her bones, the jarring of her brains as he shook not only the bed but the foundation of the house with the jackhammer of his thrusts, and, please, never again, the assault on the rosy dumpling of her cervix. He coped in his own private way in his solitary bed, and he did seem fine. Not that she would ever admit this to anyone, but there was a chance that she loved her cats unconditionally—that is, more, maybe, just a little bit more than she loved Charlie. She wasn't saying that it was true, only that it was possible. In her experience, women wanted to give and give and give, and then, suddenly, they were done, they were spent, they didn't have another crumb to offer up.

Two weeks after she'd talked to Jenna Faroli at the garden meeting, on an ordinary Wednesday night in May, she had, before dinner, still been in the early stages of her romance research, not to mention vague about who her characters would be. Making his entrance into the kitchen for his supper, Charlie, as usual, took a running start in the carpeted hall, and then slid in his stocking feet across the linoleum to the table. When they'd bought the farm, Laura had gone to considerable trouble to find the boxy refrigerator in pale green, and a speckled green-and-white Formica table, and chairs with plastic seats, so that the old farm kitchen was true to a gentler and more loving time, a period when neighbor women gathered to shell peas and put up tomatoes and pickles. Not that Laura had time for those old arts, not that she had time, these days, for friendship.

"You'll never guess," Charlie said, landing in his seat, "who I saw on my way home."

She was setting out two corn dogs for him, and a bowl of Tater Tots, baby carrots, and a glass of milk. For herself she had made a salad and a chicken patty. "Who?" she said.

"Guess."

"Give me a hint."

He didn't want to make it too easy. "A person," he said, "who never name-drops, far as I can tell."

"Take a napkin. Your sister?"

He reached for a stack of green-and-white-checked paper napkins in the crock. "Nope."

"Man or woman?"

"Woman—or hybrid, maybe. Every bit a woman but—"

"Bigger than a bread box?"

They had played this game for years. The bread-box line was standard.

"Larger, in her britches, much, than a bread box, but small enough, humble enough, to be a . . . beginner."

"Big enough in her britch—" Laura lurched across the table. "Her?" She grasped his shoulders. "You saw her?"

He was happy for any occasion when she touched him, and wished she had not so soon gone back to her own side. "Saw her! I freaking watched the Silver People with her. I flipping talked with her for at least twenty minutes." Laura did not like him to use profanity, and he did his best to avoid it in her presence. He picked up his corn dog on a stick and spoke into it. "Charles Rider and Jenna Faroli sighted a UFO convoy this afternoon on Highway S, in the township of Hartley. Ms. Faroli was skeptical at first but warmed to the idea that unidentified objects could be messengers from beyond our realm."

"You talked to her?" Mrs. Rider absently reached for a carrot. What in the world had Jenna Faroli thought of Charlie? Laura had always imagined meeting Jenna, but somehow never expected Charlie to have the experience. Did Jenna think he was insane or lovable? It could go either way, depending, and Laura couldn't always be sure what person would think which way. Was Jenna laughing at him—was she mocking him right now in the privacy of her kitchen? Charlie Rider, the ding-a-ling. "What do you mean, the Silver People?" Laura asked. "How Silver and how People-ish?" If he had told Jenna about the alien thing, she would for sure think he was certifiable.

He was tossing his Tater Tots, one by one, into the air,

and seeing if he could land them in his mouth. It was funny, how lately she was thinking about her book all the time, even when she was doing tasks that had nothing to do with it, such as watching Charlie, his head thrown back and roving side to side, his mouth wide open, his straight little top and bottom teeth bared. The question that occurred to her just then came like a stranger knocking on her door: What kind of hero would Jenna Faroli want, and, more important, need? What kind of lover? It was as if, along with the question barging in, came Jenna herself in her wide-legged Chinese silk pants and a matching wrinkled jacket, and her messy hair. It was as if she were standing there on the welcome mat waiting for Laura to decide.

Would Jenna want the Hero Devoted to a Cause? She might, since she was always interviewing people who were bent on doing good works. Or would Jenna be drawn to the Weary Warrior, someone she could mother? Or could Jenna, deep down, have a basic need for the hulk, for the Alpha, the type who'd untie her from the tracks, or in the modern-day narrative donate a kidney to her and then do the surgery himself? The manual did say it was important to have a gimmick, and Laura was partial to the Alpha Medical Doctor idea. What had initially seemed relatively simple was getting more difficult by the minute. If Laura's book was going to appeal to Every Woman, if it was going to be about Every Woman, that heroine had somehow to include the qualities of a Jenna Faroli–type intelligence.

"Charlie," Laura said firmly. "Stop that. Use your fork. Tell me. Tell me everything."

~~~~~

After dinner, she went outside to check the irrigation rig that had been giving problems in the west nursery. The air was warm and sweet, and the rising moon with its yellow cast was not stern, as it sometimes seemed on a cold winter night. She wondered again what Jenna Faroli had thought of Charlie and his cuckoo suggestion that he was the one to call if she ever had a question about extraterrestrials. She had forgotten the purpose of her walk as soon as she'd stepped outside. Her shoes were getting wet, but she didn't notice. She would later think she was behaving like Charlie, lost in her own world, forgetting what she was supposed to do, and not wearing her boots. She walked along the mowed path to the Lavender Meadow, asking herself what kind of heroine Jenna would be. Hard-core professional, naturally, but deep down was she a Wild Woman, or had she once been a Virginal Heroine? Not a virgin-virgin necessarily, but the type who is unconscious of her own passionate nature—until, that is, she's awakened by the hero. Did you have to be strict about your archetypes, Laura wondered, or could you mix and match, at least a little bit? Could you have an Earth Virgin who was wild? Would you run into trouble if you allowed the characters to stray from their archetypical traits, if you allowed them just to be themselves?

There was a list of workshops and conferences at the back

of the romance manual, and she could see now that she might possibly need some assistance. Maybe she could go to the four-day annual workshop over Labor Day at the Bear Claw Resort and Conference Center in the Wisconsin Dells, which wasn't all that far from Hartley. Years before, her family had said that she wouldn't be able to get the garden business off the ground, that she didn't know enough, didn't have the smarts, but she'd done fine. She'd figured out where to get help, and she'd had the starch to hire Charlie's sister, who had a master's degree in landscape architecture. And now she knew to sign up for a workshop, to tap into the knowledge of the experts. The workshop was months away, however, and in the meantime she thought she could get started if she could somehow channel Jenna Faroli. If she became friends with Jenna, if Jenna became a client, and then a confidante, she would tell Jenna her best and most painful stories. She'd tell her about her parents, her despicable father, the notorious wife-beater.

They'd sit on the sofa in Laura's study, both of them in stocking feet drawn under them, wrapped in shawls, drinking hot chocolate. Jenna would be amazed and horrified, but she'd understand the very human element of the situation. Laura and her siblings had never discussed the fact that their mother had killed their father. They all knew it, but they had never said it out loud to one another. Laura would tell Jenna about how, five years before his death, her father had had a stroke, and her mother, Betty, had called for an ambulance. When he got out of the hospital, when he had recovered sufficiently, he struck his wife once, twice, again, shouting that she must never humiliate him like that, not ever, letting his community see him writhing on the floor, incapacitated. She must never call 911 on him for any reason. So that when he was in danger years later, when he choked on a hard, round piece of broccoli stalk, Betty watched him clutch his throat. She watched while he gestured wildly at her. She sat still with her hands folded in her lap. She watched while he turned an unattractive, throbbing scarlet, and while he made gasping sounds, and while the color drained from his face. The change in his complexion was gradual, just as the sky's light inexorably and seamlessly dims when the sun goes down. She watched while he made the stuttering gurgles of strangulation, and she watched while he banged over onto the floor. The chair tipped, too. When she remembered it, the fall seemed to her to have occurred in slow motion and without any clattering. She watched the blank space across from her for sixty-five minutes, in order to be sure, before she called her son. No one, not her grown children, and not the men on the rescue squad, all of whom had known Laura's father, asked any questions. Laura was certain that there was no hero or heroine category, not in the romance genre, into which an author could squeeze her mother and father.

Her manual said there had to be a story question, that finding the question, or settling on the question, was the way to begin. She realized that in a roundabout way she had been asking herself, since Charlie came home that night, one essential question: what, for Jenna Faroli, would be the ideal man? The manual had said to pay attention to your itches. Laura remembered, too, that the manual stressed how important it was to do exercises to learn about your characters. She hung her arms over the fence, and picked a long grass, and chewed on it thoughtfully. She wasn't sitting in a chair smoking and drinking tea, but the fence and the grass seemed, in the moment, close approximations to her fantasy props. The pieces of the story would fall together. She didn't know why or how she knew this, but all the same she was sure. What she had to do was discover what Jenna Faroli needed, what Jenna Faroli longed for. Charlie had mentioned that he'd given Jenna his e-mail address. Laura, thinking of that, closed her eyes and saw all at once a small opening, as if in the distance. A prick of light. It was the warm, well-lit tunnel of cyberspace, and she could hear it, too, hear the scurrying, the hum of the channel that would connect Jenna and Charlie. Jenna, she realized then, would somehow come to her through Charlie. There was mystery in creating a book world, the manual had said, and she could already feel that it was so.

# Chapter 5

IN JENNA'S FIRST E-MAIL, SHE MEANT TO SAY LITTLE BEYOND the fact that she'd enjoyed meeting Charlie. She mentioned her hydrangeas, their condition the result of the former owner's neglect, and how hopeful she was that with compost, informed pruning, and a watering schedule the bushes would flourish and bloom. As she wrote, she had the sense that, although he was in the business, he was probably not someone who was interested in her shrubbery. She went on to say that she felt as if she were developing a garden fetish, that whenever she was in her office she longed to be outside. The cool air on her bare arms, she wrote, was all she wanted. Was this common in the middle-aged? she asked, as if Charlie were a doctor.

In the matter of extraterrestrials, she said she thought the impulse toward belief was driven by awe, by the wonder at how small our own lives are. She had paused while writing to listen to the frogs outside, such tiny creatures capable of making such a racket, creatures that in their habits at first seemed alien, though their calling out for love, the cry of their selves, should have been familiar. She wrote that to him, too. How many glasses of the Sena 2002 had she drunk? She didn't really wish to know Charlie Rider or to correspond with him at any length—heavens, no!—but it was neighborly to tell him she had savored the moment, standing side by side, gazing at the solar disturbances. There was, Jenna went on, something comforting about the idea of life out in the galaxy, the idea that the adventure of man, something we seemed to be botching up, was perhaps not a one-shot deal. "I assume," she said, "that your experience was not fearsome. Indeed, I hope it was not." SEND, she pressed—oh send, oh send! E-mail, she thought, was sometimes less like letter writing and more like finger painting, like a joyful, careless spattering.

On the morning after, on Thursday, she did her show about dog training, the solace of puppies, and the human brain. Jenna had two producers: Carol, who lassoed authors, actors, musicians, and politicians, those on the circuit with books, movies, or CDs; and Suzie, who was purer in her method. She tended to navigate by subject, to find ideas they should explore, and then see if there was anyone who fit the bill. Though their jobs overlapped, Suzie did more of the research, and was on hand for Jenna during the program, channeling callers to her, and alerting her to station breaks, reminding her, if the conversation strayed, to get back to a certain tack. Gary, the executive producer, usually edited the prerecorded segments, with Carol and Jenna's input. Suzie whistled through her front teeth and talked far too much about herself, and Carol could be unnervingly quiet, but Jenna had grown used to their quirks and their failings. She meant to appreciate them, and she tried to reward their efforts and loyalty. She also put a good deal of energy into mentoring the young people who came through doing internships or those in their first jobs. It was her hope that none of them would have to fight power-hungry prima donnas and timid, intractable administrators, as she had had to do when she was coming up. She did like the idea of herself as the grande dame, she who was incapable of being threatened, she who welcomed and nurtured the next crop.

"That was less of a stretch, puppies to the brain pan, than I thought it would be," Jenna said to the two women after the show.

"We had spaniels when I was little," Suzie said. "My father had our favorite put down, no explanation. That was when I realized I was never going to forgive him."

"Suzie," Carol said, "you've lost weight. Stand up once. Your ass is about four times smaller than it was three weeks ago."

"Twelve pounds so far," Suzie said.

"It's because we see you every day," Carol said, "that we hadn't noticed." Carol was small and trim, with a crew cut and a wandering eye, her distinguishing feature. Suzie had frizzy blond hair, the physical manifestation, she always said, of being ADHD.

"The thing I'm doing—it's an effective diet." Suzie was shuffling through her papers as she spoke. "I'm going for another twenty. It's about time, don't you think? How long can you hate your body? How long do you battle your self-esteem issues? Maybe you just can't go on forever being a fatso and complaining about it."

The fact that Suzie had not been talking about this so-called diet of hers, the fact that she had lost twelve pounds in silence, made Jenna suspicious. It is, after all, a universal truth that women lose weight when they fall in love. Suzie, Jenna realized, had been wearing thin V-neck T-shirts—that was what was different about her. Suzie had been showing off her breasts. So, if Mrs. Raditz was having an affair, at some point Jenna and Carol and the engineer, Pete, would suffer from her suffering, even if Suzie didn't tell directly. There would be crying in the bathroom, there would be unexplained running from her cubicle, there would be no whistling in the hallway. Leave it to Suzie to make something that drove them all crazy into a habit they'd miss.

"What time tomorrow," Jenna said, "are we calling Al?"

"Ten-fifteen," Carol said. "That's all set. And, Suzie, you got the author of the book about multiple births, about fertility technology, for Tuesday, right?"

"She's on board. I've got the book for you, Jenna. It will

be clear, after you take a look at it, that people should only be allowed to have babies by screwing. Night screwing, day screwing, round-the-clock screwing. By breaking their headboards, by falling out of bed. If you can't beget a kid without screwing, adopt. No more assisted reproductive technology allowed."

"I'll be sure to bring that up with the author," Jenna said. "I'm sure saying so won't offend anyone."

On Friday, for fifteen minutes, she spoke by phone with Al Gore. In the studio she had a scientist from the Climate System Research Center, as well as an emeritus professor of meteorology, an expert on hurricanes, a global-warming naysayer. It was the type of show she least enjoyed, the sort of program that could so easily turn into a shouting match. The phone lines had gone berserk after the professor had said that chemicals and pesticides had helped make our nation the safest, the healthiest in the world. From her seat in Studio B, Jenna looked through the picture window into the next room, where Pete Warner managed the control desk, and Suzie, at her computer, screened the callers. Suzie had a knack for ferreting out the toxic and the schizophrenics, and in addition she could anticipate Jenna's thinking, often sending her a caller who would give the show a forward movement. It was when Suzie was separated from her by glass, and in the heat of the moment, that Jenna felt at one with her. Separated by glass, Jenna loved frizzy-haired, buxom, gap-toothed ADHD Suzie Raditz.

After the climate show, Jenna closed her office door, took her headache medication, and began her weekend rereading of short stories by a woman she called "the Saint." It was her proudest accomplishment, to have finally snagged an interview with the woman she considered to be the greatest living writer. She had forgotten about her Wednesday-evening e-mail to Charlie Rider, had not, in fact, thought twice about a response from him. On Saturday, she sat on the porch at home all morning and into the afternoon reading through the Saint's collections, alternately terrified and thrilled at the prospect of Monday's interview. She would have been no more nervous, she said to Frank, if she'd been called upon to interview Virginia Woolf or Henry James.

"You'll be terrific," he'd said. "She'll love you."

"I'm not after love," she said. "I just want to do her justice."

"When are you not terrific?"

Would that every woman had a friend in her corner like Frank. Jenna had kissed her husband's freckled summer pate, and gone upstairs to check her mail. Who would have written her in the hours she'd been away? What delightful communication awaited?

"Charlie Rider?" she said out loud. She hoped she would not have to write him back; that was her first thought. She hoped he was writing a simple thank-you for her thank-you, and that would be the end of it. She remembered, already with a pang of regret, that she'd written to him more soulfully than she should have.

Subj: Highway S
From: crider@kingmail.com
To: JFaroli@wis.staff.edu

Dear Jenna (if I may):

Might I say that I have always admired you? Your warmth and energy have been a bright spot in my day for years now, in the potting shed, in the car, in the kitchen. You are a light (but not a supernatural one) that has followed me from home, to work, and back again. You might be tired of people telling you what you mean to them but it would require more discipline than I have not to speak from my heart. I feel that you do not judge people, and so I feel safe telling you about my first encounter with those beings I have always called the Silver People. I was eighteen. It was a Saturday night in midsummer. Petie Druzinsky, Bill Mabbit, and I were walking through Doc Webster's back forty. You will assume that we were under the influence but I swear to you we weren't. We hadn't had a puff, a swig, nothing. As clear-minded as usual, which I admit is not all that crystal clear. We experienced an unbearable light coming toward us. All of us remembered being in the grip of it. None of us can explain what happened during the four hours that we can't account for. Was it real? Did it happen? I no longer know. I say to myself that *it only happened because I perceived it happening, but I also am willing to believe there are whole realms, entire realities, that we are not aware of. Because of that incident, Petie Druzinsky found Jesus. Bill drinks more than he should and will not talk much about our experience. He blames his troubles—bad marriage, drunkenness, inability to hold down a job—on that night. As I said, I believe it, I don't believe it, I believe it, I don't believe it. If I were to believe in anything, though, it is that the Silver People arranged for us to meet. There was a light around you on the pavement. My wife tells me I exaggerate, that I see things, but let me say that the light, the bluish light, seemed holy. Whatever or whoever or even if no one arranged our meeting, it was lovely to share whatever it was, with you.*

*Very sincerely,*
*Charlie Rider*


"No wonder!" Jenna said, laughing. If Charlie had seen her shrouded in a holy light, he could easily believe he'd had an encounter with aliens. She, the virgin, humble, submissive, incurious. She laughed again. She imagined the three boys in the field standing before—what? What had it been that would overpower three teenagers on a summer night? And she thought, Anything at all. Anything could happen to the young, which was part of the sadness of growing older. No one, not even an alien, would want to abduct Jenna, and, perhaps more to the point, even if a human-sized toad with language skills from Planet Z happened to be at the door, Jenna would not give it the time of day. There were enough problems on earth without having to scavenge for more heartache out in the universe.

She went back then, to the Saint's stories, to those heroines who were often as wise as God but trapped by their erotic natures. *This is a persistent theme in your work, dear Saint.* She had begun her list of comments and questions:

1. Your females often swing between two states—indeterminacy and male mastery—no middle ground for them, no other modes of being.

2. Do you think feminism has made it easier for women to negotiate the pitfalls of romantic love and marriage?

3. Your stories have moments of radiance, but the fantasies are always provisional. Why is character after character charmed by excess even as they long for balance and wholeness?

4. Why are your women nearly always led astray by their obsessions for crazy or infantile or difficult or cruel men, men they can neither be with nor escape?

# Chapter 6

IT HAD BEEN A DELAYED SPRING, AND WHEN THE WINDS CHANGED
and the air warmed, the trees budded and bloomed in swift
succession, magnolia to redbud to apple to lilac, a suspended
time of fragrance, and migrating birds singing early and late.
Jenna realized that in her suburban life of lawn mowing and
bush trimming, administered by Yard Care Inc., she had lost
the sense of headlong rush, the race: grass and weed and root
and vine vying to be biggest, the most lush, to spread the far-
thest. She hoped to make a small, quiet garden by the porch
with spiky purple salvias and fluffy pink astilbe, and a touch
of golden coreopsis, to dazzle the coolness of the composition.
She had been reading garden books and felt she was learning
the lingo, just as she and Frank, years before, had acquired the
wine-tasting jargon. In the shady wooded corner, she wanted
the delicate, starlike flowers of sweet woodruff and the frothy

white rodgersia, and, behind, the black snakeroot, and the queen-of-the-prairie—all of it to be sublimely thought out and lovingly tended. And then the rest of their acreage, fields and woods, could go as wild and tangled as it pleased. She wrote about nature's competitive abandon to Charlie, and he e-mailed back, "Lust is everywhere in front of you and I."

She meant to be subtle rather than schoolmarmish in her grammar correction. "I'm not sure if the blush and burst of spring," she rhapsodized, "in front of you and me is lust as much as desire."

In the two weeks before they met for the second time, there were thirty-seven messages between them. A few were paragraph-length, but most were short, a line or two, including among them three LOLs. That was the extent of their wish to abbreviate. Neither of them used emoticons. She later thought that if he'd used them she would not have continued to write him. She could not take anyone seriously who littered his communications with smiley faces and frowns, the exchanges seemingly written by a primary-school teacher to her charges. Jenna would rather her correspondents have been abducted by aliens than resort to picturegraphs, to colons and parentheses to express themselves.

She hadn't planned for an epistolary relationship with him, but when he'd written her back, telling her about the night in the field, she had felt compelled to say a few more words. She was suspended, she said in her second message, in a pocket between disbelief and belief, as perhaps he was, a space made possible, finally, by being in her forties. She was now able to hold two opposing views in her head and see virtue and meaning in both—a trick youth hadn't afforded her.

If she was writing to Charlie Rider so earnestly, it was because she remembered a quality of striving in him; it was that quality to which she spoke. She had no doubt, she'd assured him, that he was telling the truth, and even if memory and experience itself weren't always to be trusted, there wasn't much else a person could do but trust the fragments, the distortions, the longing that is memory.

He had written back a rhyme:

*Subj: Tartoli*
*From: crider@kingmail.com*
*To: JFaroli@wis.staff.edu*

*Jenna Faroli, Queen of Tartoli,*
*The muse of Men, Women, and Mice,*
*She sings, she dances, she makes pasta e fagioli,*
*She's smarter than Jesus H. Christ.*

There were eleven more stanzas, each beginning with her name, each in the same spirit of encomium, ending with:

*Jenna Faroli, the Dame of the Bandwidth,*
*Knows not how the world loves her voice.*
*Beyond all her kin, beyond all her kith,*
*Ninety-point-four FM is the choice.*

"I am sure," she replied, "that no one has ever before rhymed bandwidth with kith. This poem is the closest thing made for me that sounds like it has been, but in fact was not, written by Dr. Seuss. I am going to render it in counted cross-stitch and hang it on my office wall."

Jenna received two hundred e-mails a day at work, and was not in need of more correspondents. She had three accounts, one of which Suzie vetted, and another for in-house station business, and, last, her private address, which of late had been flooded by her daughter. Vanessa was working on her doctorate at Washington University in St. Louis, and she called her mother every day, in addition to writing her, sometimes hourly. Her study of postsynaptic 5-HT receptors and offensive aggression in rats was turning out literally to be a rat race. There were other troubles as well, including the two boyfriends in the last year who had proved to be enormous jerks, and there were the inconsiderate housemates, and quarrels with the lab technician. There was no end of misery for Vanessa, and Jenna was ever poised to listen and offer what little solace she could. She had come to dread the phone ringing at home, because she knew that whatever Vanessa was going to complain about was news that Jenna would then have to carry with her, another piece of unhappiness that daughter had carelessly unloaded on mother.

She had had Vanessa when she was twenty-two, ten months after her marriage to Frank, because she'd been told she would have trouble conceiving. The child bride got knocked up immediately, but in delivery her uterus had ruptured, nearly killing her and the baby. That Jenna had had a hysterectomy at such a young age was a great sadness in her otherwise lucky life. She often wished, when Vanessa called, that there were sisters for her to phone instead of the one helpless and perhaps overly indulgent and involved mother. Vanessa could have used a phalanx of siblings to absorb her complaints, but her busy parents had put off adopting, and finally it had been too late.

Charlie's e-mails amid all the chatter were less of an annoyance than Jenna might have admitted. She knew she should have been irritated by them, she who, like many of her contemporaries, felt that e-mail had robbed her blind, stealing hours that could have been spent reading. E-mail, she often said, had ruined her life, and yet there were always those most seductive questions in her approach to her desk: who would have written? What astonishing morsel, what wisdom, what battling wit might there be at the click of the mouse? It was out of largesse, she told herself at first, that she was writing to a stranger in Hartley, a stranger who did not always observe the rules of grammar—although, in fairness, he had used *pasta e fagioli* in a rhyme with ease. She might come from the studio to her office after a show to find a message from him, a bit of whimsy, or flattery so outrageous she actually did laugh out loud. What did it matter if he didn't always use *good* and *well* correctly? Why should she judge? She knew enough people who were so vigilant about the use of the English language it was dangerous to speak to them.

If her replies were acerbic, he seemed amused rather than offended. And when he was contrite about something he'd said, he was abjectly solemn about his error. She once signed off as "The Dame of the Bandwidth," and he'd fired back with "FUCKING A!" Five minutes later his moniker reappeared:

Subj: I'm so sorry
From: crider@kingmail.com
To: JFaroli@wis.staff.edu

Dear Jenna,
    Please forgive me for being a crass idiot. I should not have said F***ing A. It was so very crude. Please forgive me. I do hope you can forgive me.

She replied:

Subj: Re: I'm so sorry
From: JFaroli@wis.staff.edu
To: crider@kingmail.com

Dear Crass Fucking Idiot,

The Silver People will smite you.

And he returned with:

_Laura Rider's Masterpiece_

Subj: Re: I'm so sorry
From: crider@kingmail.com
To: JFaroli@wis.staff.edu

Dame Bandwidth—

I _am_ smitten.

She did not feel as if she were flirting with him, not really, nor he with her. That was impossible. She had succumbed to the silly exchange, and it was playful, that was all. She did not often feel a sexual charge, a condition she blamed on her hysterectomy, and she could also blame her hectic life. She and Frank had become accustomed to perpetual motion and perpetual exhaustion. Her private sadness had been with her so long, was so much a part of her, that she would have had a hard time separating the pure foundation of herself from the sorrow. At twenty-two, she had been rendered barren—such a desolate, awful word—and there was the other difficult piece, the fact of Frank's indifference to her sexually after the crisis of Vanessa's birth. Jenna had lost her drive, but he seemed not to mind. She had thought in the beginning that he was being careful with her, of his girlish wife who had been close to death, was nursing a squalling infant, recovering from major surgery, and suffering from mastitis in both breasts. Hormone therapy did not restore her passionate nature, but even when, out of consideration, she offered him the opportunity, he took up his book or made a halfhearted attempt.

For some time, that absence in their lives plagued her. He was fifteen years older, pushing the advanced age of forty, and she wondered if he suddenly could have become impotent but was too embarrassed to say. Maybe he had not ever loved her physically, maybe in courtship he had put on a show of ardor and worship out of love for everything else about her, or maybe the bloated pustule of her mother-self was a permanent turnoff. Maybe at a simple biological level he could find no reason to couple with a *barren* woman. Had she always been undesirable—was that it? She realized that he'd from the start treated her in a fatherly way, something she didn't want to ponder too deeply. Was he having an affair? No, his probity was unquestionable, and even if he'd been the type to have a woman on the side, his schedule would prohibit a dalliance.

They had not had success talking about the problem. They seemed unable to muster the strength to begin, or if the thought of what they'd given up made her weep Frank became nervous and irritable. While men and women everywhere were discussing their sexual dysfunction, on the street, on television, and in print, she and Frank were silent on the subject. They were always racing in and out, they adored Vanessa, they were fond of each other and devoted, and beyond their routine and the life of the mind, what they shared, Jenna believed, was their unspoken grief.

She knew, certainly, that there were greater sorrows in life. She had done her best to rout out bitterness and focus her energy on her work. She, Jenna Faroli of the sexy mind, was satisfied that if the multitudes wanted to fuck her, it was her brain they wanted to penetrate, the luscious cranial fruit on those broad shoulders of hers—what hidden folds, so soft, so moist, so yielding. She considered that big fruit, and then the rest of her, the drag of her body, to be the ultimate product of the feminist revolution. She more or less had it all, as promised: terrific job, caring husband, healthy daughter, and the bonus of public adulation. Not least, she'd managed to avoid the sniper shots of her co-workers as she rose up in the ranks.

～

She had mentioned to Charlie a few days ahead of time that she was planning to stop at Prairie Wind Farm on the upcoming Saturday morning. And though she expected to see him at some point in the venture, she was not thinking, as she opened her car door in the small parking lot, that he'd appear at her side as if he'd been dropped from above. She let out a shriek.

"Oh, honey!" He gripped her elbow. "I'm so sorry." He was wearing what looked like a farmer costume, blue-and-white-striped overalls, a light-blue chambray shirt, and a cap to match.

"Jesus," she breathed. "Where'd you come from?"

"I've been told I was spawned by a fish. A trout, I always thought."

"You must have gotten your eyes from the father," Jenna

said. "A creature who was unrelated to the ichthyoids. Bovine, I'd say. A trout and a bull coupled to make Charlie Rider."

"And you," he said, "you were—"

"Adopted. My birth mother was one of those girls who were sent to homes far, far away to have their bastard babies. This occurred before shame went out of style." His great lashed eyes widened, and she laughed at him. "I know what you're thinking."

"What? What exactly am I thinking?"

"You're thinking that I have been liberated to invent my parents. They can be washerwoman and prince, they can be slave and master, they can be anything else besides a desperate sixteen-year-old girl and a boy who was going off to the army. At least, that's what I would think if I were you."

"Doesn't everything," he said, looking at her slantwise, "depend on how you tell it?"

"You are extremely dangerous," she said. "You don't forget a word. I am going to shop rather than speak to you."

He stood in her way, would not let her pass. "But who," he said plaintively, "raised you?"

"A childless middle-aged couple. Remote father, distracted mother. Maybe parenthood hadn't been the dream-come-true, after all. Both with high expectations. I was lonely and bookish, went to boarding school, and then to college. Very Victorian, you could say. The parents, the four of them, as far as I know, are dead." She stepped to the side of him. "May I purchase some blooms now, please?"

She had come to buy whatever he would recommend to set along the path to the woods. She wanted wispy flowers that would grow tall and fall over. Dame's rocket was supposed to be an evil, invasive weed, but she wanted a brilliant stand of anything that would run rampant. She had been thinking in the last day or two that instead of ordered beds she wanted a mess; she wanted riot and indelicacy. She had not planned to make a morning of this errand, and when he offered a tour of the farm, a stroll to the Lavender Meadow, a walk in the forest, she said, "Yes, yes," in a distracted way, hoping they would hurry.

Off they went along a path with black iris in bloom, a blossoming sage, yellow iris with orange centers, and a long row of peonies going from pink to red to dark red. He opened a wooden lattice gate, and they climbed mossy steps to a line of birch trees planted in parallel form. The fractured sunlight wavered on the grass, the slim, straight birches were nymphish and regal, and there was nothing in the distant opening but pale-green rye swaying in the wind. The world behind them was fading. She tried to speak but found she could not. "Charlie," she croaked so softly he did not hear her. She wanted him to wait, but he had turned a corner into what could only be called a room, a group of small apple trees, and underneath them a wooden table and two chairs.

"Charlie!" she tried again. No one had told her about the beauty of this place, about the simplicity of its charm. No one had warned her. He did seem to understand that she was stricken, and so he kindly said nothing. They went down a mowed path into another sanctuary, this one an old cherry orchard, the thick limbs gnarled, the ancient bark papery and peeling. Someone else would have cut down the trees, but the mastermind here had studied the elemental Gertrude Jekyll, and a host of others, Penelope Hobhouse, Edith Wharton and the Italian villas, Bunny Williams, Tasha Tudor, Beatrice Farrand, and perhaps even the godly Olmsted himself. There was nothing overly rusticated, nothing cute or cluttered or studied or pretentious. They came to a terraced pond with chipped Tuscan oil jars defining the entry, fieldstone walls around the beds of lady ferns, meadow rue, soapwort, and forget-me-nots. When Jenna touched the top of the wall, Charlie muttered, "One fuc— I mean, one stone at a time." She wished he had not spoken, but then the fact of his labor came to her, Charlie, alone, building the perilous wall, rock chinked to rock, one after another, his tendrils falling into his eyes.

Jenna was unaccustomed to being speechless. She was sure he sensed her awe, and perhaps he could tell that, as much as their silence was a part of the wonder of it, she did also want to understand how, rock after rock, the place had been made. As they went on, he now and again quietly pointed out a structural challenge, or he explained what the hillside had looked like when they'd arrived. At first he gave all the credit to Laura, for seeing the potential, for giving the farm what amounted to a makeover. He had merely done the grunt work, he said; he had merely followed her commands. But then, trailing his hand on the wall, he said, "I've never told anyone this—I would never tell *her*—but there were times when I disobeyed orders, because I knew that from an engineering standpoint—and sometimes even visually—I knew that she was wrong. There are tokens all over of my adjustments which for whatever reason we never mention."

"That's nice," Jenna murmured.

They climbed another set of steps that led to the field of lavender—an acre of romance, he called it—that Laura had planted on a whim. Jenna would have liked to fall into the flowers, into the windy softness of the smell; she wanted to climb into the field itself, to be of it somehow. She wanted—she wanted—she hardly knew what. She turned to look at Charlie, to try to see in him how Laura Rider, the pretty, glassy-eyed woman who had not seemed forceful, had held all of this in her head, and urged it into being.

"It's good, isn't it?" he said.

She could only nod. If the three boys had been abducted by aliens, then why not say a spell had been cast upon her, rendering her mute and yet also happy. It was a feeling that was only slightly disturbed when they came out—after how long? an hour? two!—back to the barn where the plants were sold, where several Hispanic men were watering potted perennials on planks. There was no sign of Mrs. Rider.

She had felt at peace with Charlie in the quiet, walking through the woodland hallways, breathing together, smelling the mossy undergrowth, the sweet decaying loam. She was not, she would have said, accustomed to peace. She'd had the oddest sense that she was a girl again, that she was with a boy roaming the forest in a childhood she hadn't ever had. She'd wanted to take his hand. In his overalls and cap he seemed a boy at play, a boy who could show her things that, for all her experience, she had not known were in the world.

# Chapter 7

AT THE RIDER HOUSE, THE FIRST COMMUNICATION FROM
Jenna had been a giddy occasion. Charlie had been in his office when the message came through. "At my desk," he later
said to Jenna, "waiting for you." He was in the nook upstairs, watching Jerry Lewis and Dean Martin clips on You-
Tube, when JFaroli@wis.staff.edu appeared. They had met
on Highway S that same afternoon, four hours earlier. "You
wrote me!" he said. In a whisper he read the letter: " 'There
is something comforting about the idea of alien life forms'—
Yep," he agreed, "there is—'in fiction, in nonfiction, and in
life, the idea that the adventure of man, something we seem
to be botching up, is perhaps not a one-shot deal.' " He said
again, "Yep." And "You really get it, JFaroli."

Charlie Rider was capable of being a decisive person. He
felt what he felt and he knew what he felt. He already knew

that he loved Jenna Faroli—that is, as a person. He loved
her voice, her open mind, and her coiffure. Not that it
would happen, but in the event that it did, say, in the next
life, he knew he would love her form. He would have no
problem unbuttoning her shirt, one pearl button at a time,
and kissing her small, high bosoms. He loved the way she'd
gotten out of the car and spoken without looking at him,
as if they'd been friends for years, as if they always met on
the shoulder of the road, as if they'd always had the bond of
that place on Highway S. He loved how, clearly, she didn't
think she was beautiful, and how she didn't care if her hair
was falling out of the fifteen barrettes that looked as if she'd
stapled them to her scalp. He loved how she'd probably
been speaking to the President that day, or Steven Spiel-
berg, and how she'd given Charlie the same consideration
as the big shots.

"It was a pleasure to meet you," she had concluded in her
e-mail.

"I love you," he said to the screen.

He printed out the message and bounded down the stairs
with it. "She wrote me," he called. "Laura! Where are you?
She wrote me!" It did not, at this point, occur to him to sup-
press the information.

His wife was back from her walk, from checking the irrigation rig, and had settled in her study, in the room Charlie had made for her when they'd bought the place. He'd
ripped out the paneling, and made shelves for her books,

her videos, and her collection of troll dolls, and he'd laid down hardwood that he'd salvaged from his uncle's shop. At her bidding he'd painted the walls orange, a hot contemporary color that made him feel as if he were lying in the blazing sun with his eyes closed. It seemed doubtful it would suit her for her quiet moods, and at the paint store he'd asked the clerk to mix in a mere suggestion of white to cool it down. It was his small secret with the walls. She had a drafting table where she sketched her garden designs, and a desk for the paperwork, and a daybed for her reading. When he came through the door, she had her elbows on her desk, her hands at her cheeks, and she was staring at a thick plastic-coated library book. She looked up at him as if—for an instant—she didn't recognize him. "What?" she said. "What'd you say?"

"Jenna. Jenna Faroli. JFaroli at wis dot staff dot e-d-u. She, she fucking wrote to me."

The first thought that came to Laura was this: Jenna must not think Charlie is insane if she's writing him only hours after she's met him. "That's great," she said. He was wearing her plush pink bathrobe dotted with fat white sheep. "That's—incredible." He handed her the paper. "Don't say *fucking*," she said as she skimmed the message. She stilled herself and began again at the beginning. When she was done, she set the page aside, smoothing it with her fingers. "Now," she said to her husband, "now we have to write her back."

"I know." He had begun to jiggle, the thing he did that started in his knees, the spazzing that made his thighs wobble. "I know, I was just going to—"

"We have to think what to say." She opened her laptop. "We shouldn't send it back instantly, though, that's for sure. We should wait a few days." He was eager, she could see, but she knew he was capable of being patient. He was like a good dog in that respect. She felt sorry for Muslim women in strict Islamic countries, sorry for submissive females, because if they were married to the Arabic version of Charlie it would be far more difficult to get things done. Under her direction, he had slaved away at realizing her vision for the farm. He had dug holes and hauled boulders and built fences and planted trees and pulled thistles. He would not, however, reroof the barn, because he was afraid of heights. She would never have asked it of him. "Charlie," she said, "there's this feeling I have."

"What feeling?" His wife, the realist, did not often have *feelings*, but when she did, all of a sudden Charlie was buying a farm, or plowing up a field for lavender, or hiring an old lady who'd seemed unlikely but would prove to be invaluable. Laura's feelings were like dowsing rods.

"I think," Laura said slowly, "I think that you and Jenna should be friends."

He stopped jiggling. "How do you mean?"

"I think maybe she moved to Hartley for this reason."

"What reason?"

"To get to know you. It might sound nutty, but—"

"To get to know me?" He pictured the stage again, the Grand Ole Opry, he and Jenna singing together with their backup girls. And then he saw the two of them standing on a hillside looking across fields and rivers and lakes, watching as the night velveted the sky, the stars one by one twinkling down at them. "Don't you bet she's busy all the time?" He said this wistfully.

"There's nobody like you," his wife said matter-of-factly. That Charlie was one of a kind was the truest thing she could say about him. When they'd first met, she couldn't stop taking pictures of him, and even though he had worn her out, she still thought he was beautiful. She remembered the way he'd used to look at her, the way the strength of his love, the love itself, she thought, had made his eyes wet and glossy. She knew she was getting ahead of herself, but she had to wonder what Jenna would think of Charlie, if a man like Charlie, that is, happened to aim his watery beams on her.

Laura would have said that the first message was a collaborative effort, that if you had to talk in percentages her contribution was in the high seventies, and Charlie's somewhere in the twenties. Charlie, she guessed, would probably come to imagine he'd written the entire thing, and that would be all right with her, it really would.

" 'Dear Jenna (if I may):' "—Laura spoke as she wrote— " 'Might I say that I have always admired you? Your warmth and energy have been a bright spot in my day for years now, in the potting shed, in the car, in the kitchen.'" She paused, taking satisfaction that the voice sounded nicely self-effacing and complimentary, that it sounded enough like Charlie's bull, and that in addition the content was Laura's true feeling. Not bad. "Do we put a smiley face?"

Charlie, forearms on the desk, his small, taut rear in the air, leaned into her. "No. She wouldn't like it." He was sure of this. "She likes words." He read over what Laura had written and said, "What if Jenna quizzes me on her programs? I never listen to what she's saying, I only hear how she's saying it."

"She's not going to quiz you." Laura typed on in quiet for a minute. "'You might be tired,'" she started up again, "'of people telling you what you mean to them but it would re-quire more . . . discipline than I have not to speak from my heart.' That's good! That's great." She could feel Charlie press-ing into her side. "Do you want to tell her about the night with Petie Druzinksy and Bill Mabbit?" As if to herself she said, "I think so. I think you do."

"It has to be right, it has to be told in just the—"

"You don't want to make it sound too far out, like you were completely changed by it, like it wrecked your life. You want to make it seem like you could go either way, like it happened but maybe it didn't happen."

"Which is pretty much accurate," he said. "Most of the time I think that."

"How you sound depends on who you're talking to. When

you're in the UFO chat room, there's no question." Laura had read over his shoulder once when he was online with the paranormal group, and she'd gotten so spooked, so afraid that the spaceship was going to return for Charlie, that she'd ended up taking a Valium.

"I want to tell it—" he tried. "She said to tell—"

" 'All of us,' " Laura was writing, " 'experienced an unbearable light come toward us. All of us remembered being . . . in the grip of it.' " She drew back to study her message. "Yes!" she said. "The grip of it!"

She took a deep breath, filling her lungs with the muskiness of Charlie's deodorant, the mint of his toothpaste, the lavender of their bath soap. There was no trace of just plain man; hard to say whether Jenna would approve of his dueling layers, or if she was the kind who would try to sniff down to the original stink of Charlie himself.

"The grip of it," he repeated. Maybe that was all right. Maybe that was how it had been. He wanted Jenna to know it was real. He wanted her to understand how the light itself had picked him up, how he had been carried into something that wasn't so much a place as a feeling. Not a Laura-type feeling, but the Charlie type. If you had to call it a place, it was like the inside of an egg, a smooth, transparent shell, warm and empty, beautiful, maybe, and terrible, too. At first he'd never been so alone.

Laura was typing furiously: " 'If I were to believe in anything, though, it is that the Silver People arranged for us to meet.'"

That was fine, Charlie thought, that was the truth. "Tell her," he cried, "that she glowed. Because she did. She had a halo in the afternoon light."

"Not *glow*! That sounds like she was radioactive. 'There was a light,'" Laura wrote, "'around you on the pavement. My wife,'" she continued, "'tells me I exaggerate, that I see things, but let me say that the light, the bluish light, seemed holy.'" She wrinkled her nose. "That's laying it on heavy, but it is how you'd describe it."

"Say"—he was bouncing now, on his toes—"say, 'You might not believe me, but it's a fact. And say, 'Whatever or whoever got us together, it was great to meet you.'"

"'Whatever or whoever,'" Laura typed, "'or even if no one arranged our meeting, it was . . . it was lovely to share whatever it was, with you.' She'll be surprised, I'll bet, and pleased, that you used the word *lovely*. Women like it when men use certain flowery words."

"Okay," Charlie said.

"Oh my gosh." Laura's hands froze on the keyboard.

"What?" Charlie bent over so he was looking up into her unblinking eyes. "What's the matter?"

"Shush!" The understanding had come to her, a flash, so clear and then—gone. How to get it back? It was something about how her two fantasies were linked. They were linked, yes, because—because Laura's notion that Jenna Faroli was her teacher and her daydream that she was an author were two parts of the same picture. Yes, yes! She could not be an author without Jenna, because Jenna was the guide into her book. That was what she had begun to see out in the Lavender Meadow: it was Jenna Faroli who would lead her up the glass mountain. All these years, Laura's waking fantasies had seemed separate, but they were like Siamese twins, sharing organs, feeding off each other, the same blood flowing through the bodies.

"What's the matter?" Charlie said again.

"Lovely," she murmured. "I think Jenna already knows you're not the average man, and so she'll really appreciate the word *lovely*." She stared not at her husband but at the screen. What category of hero was Charlie? Dreamer, yes; underdog, yes; artist, yes; bonkers, yes. She said, "How do we want to sign off?"

"Yours truly?"

"Yours truly—no. How about sincerely? 'Yours truly' sounds stuffy. 'Sincerely' sounds more . . . sincere."

"How about 'very sincerely'?"

"You always have to slather it on, don't you?" She sighed. So let him have his way; let Jenna know he was both prone to excess and *very* sincere. Laura read the message through, stopping to change a word, to glance heavenward in thought, and back to the screen to correct the corrections. "I like it," she pronounced at last. "I'm going to e-mail this to you, and then you send it to her. But wait a few days. She's busy, like you said, and you don't want to be pushy."

He had gone quiet, a dangerous sign, a sign that meant he was thinking.

"Charlie," she said softly, "she'll be a great—a lovely friend for you."

# Chapter 8

BECAUSE JENNA AND FRANK LIVED OFF THE BEATEN PATH IN
a place that seemed exotic to urbanites, and because through
the years they had accumulated friends from all over the world,
they often had houseguests. They considered themselves rich
in good company, and they were usually not unhappy to host
their visitors for two days—three at the outside. The week
after Jenna's woodland stroll at Prairie Wind Farm, Dickie,
a former poet laureate, and his wife, Sally, the hematologist,
came to stay for the weekend. Jenna and the poet began their
Saturday morning sitting at the edge of her beginner's garden
in the floral lawn chairs that the former occupants had left
behind. The chairs were too ugly to keep and too comfortable
to discard, which in the future would be a problem in relation to the yard's composition, when the fledgling plants took
hold and became magnificent.

Jenna and Dickie lounged next to each other, faces to the sun, as if they were on a cruise ship. Dickie was older than Jenna by twelve years, but his silky hair, which was still dark, and his small rectangular glasses, now back in fashion, made him seem nearly as youthful as he'd been when she'd met him, when she herself had been eighteen. He was Frank's friend, but from the start, from their first dinner, there was no one she liked to talk to as much as Dickie Karmauth. In fact, she sometimes thought that Frank married her in large part because she fell into step so naturally with Dickie and Sally, his two essential pals. Dickie was a charming melancholic and, as Frank did, he knew everything, although his categories of everything were different.

In the garden that morning, they discussed a biography they'd recently read of Leonard Woolf, which led to the predictable Bloomsbury tangents: their wish to visit the many sites, Sissinghurst and Charleston and Monk's House; the work that was still circulating by Duncan Grant, available for purchase at a New York gallery; and Dickie's eternal thanks to Jenna for a long-ago gift she'd given him, a sketch of Dora Carrington's she'd found in London. It had been years since Dickie had recited the opening of *To the Lighthouse* to her, something he'd learned because it was the only book he'd had with him the summer he was stranded for two weeks on the Isle of Rassay, off the coast of Scotland.

" 'Yes, of course,' " Dickie began, " 'if it's fine tomorrow,' " said Mrs. Ramsay. 'But you'll have to be up with the lark,' she added."

Jenna closed her eyes, letting the sun do its damage, and listened. Virginia Woolf seemed to have perfect recall of how it felt to be a child, to be a boy with the prospect of an expedition, a boy in love with his mother, a boy filled with joy. Jenna, as always, was grateful for Dickie's classy brain and generous heart. When he recited, Dickie himself receded, so that the work shone out, something that was not true when Frank spewed his soliloquies. The poet on the surface was softer, mellower than Judge Voden, but within he was tortured, although in a refined way. When he had his dark days, he went to his woodland cabin and read and listened to music and felt, he sometimes said, suicidal, but, he was quick to assure his friends, pleasantly so. His voice now was low and lulling. She wished he would recite *To the Lighthouse* all day long, recite as she fell asleep and stayed asleep, dreaming to the rhythms of Woolf's sentences. An hour ago, she had gotten out of bed, but it didn't matter that already she was limp and warm and drowsy. It was funny that, when she pictured the little boy in the book, James Ramsay, getting ready to go on his trip to the lighthouse, she imagined a young Charlie Rider. A delicate boy with brown eyes and curls, a boy who at first was quivering with anticipation.

When she woke, for in fact she did fall asleep, the trees were shading her face, and she was covered with a thin blanket— the work of Dickie. Her guests were in the kitchen watching

Frank pour a mixture of butter and lemon juice over the leg of lamb. Sally was saying to him, "Sweetheart, you're caring for that slab of meat as if it's a kitten."

"I love it more than a cat," he murmured into the roasting pan.

They were already drinking gin-and-tonics, although they had not yet eaten lunch. The afternoon would drift by them as they grazed and wandered from topic to topic. Frank would play the piano, accompanying Sally through her repertory of eighteenth-century Italian love songs. That Jenna wasn't musical had probably been a disappointment to Frank, but she couldn't help her failure. She'd been told in grade-school chorus to mouth the words, to make sure she didn't actually sing. Frank, the Renaissance man, the overachiever, had minored in piano performance, and had not given up his chamber groups during law school. His greatest pleasures through the years had been accompanying Sally, and also making their daughter study the violin so he could play sonatas with her. Dickie and Frank, both single children who had adopted each other as sibling, had known Sally in college. There had been, apparently, a brief rivalry between the men over Sally, but she had resolved it for them, choosing Dickie while managing, nonetheless, to keep Frank close. Frank had never said, but Jenna knew that it had taken him years to get over his friend's wife, the doctor, the soprano, the elegant blonde who still wore her hair in a French twist, the woman who had chosen the difficult poet with the silky hair over the balding man of great reason.

That morning, Sally and Frank had spent half an hour cracking open a hundred cardamom pods, after which he'd pulverized the seeds in the coffee grinder. He had approved the waxy cover of fat on the lamb and the soft purple muscle underneath; they all had been required to pay their respects. The windows and doors were wide open, and the fragrance of the roast in the mild June breeze added to their happiness. Midafternoon, they had ended up on the porch, deep into the wicker chairs, each with a book nearby, although no one was reading. Frank said to the guests, "Did Jenna mention that she saw a squadron of UFOs outside of Hartley?"

"Lucky!" Dickie said.

"Dickie's the only person in the world who wants more than anything to have an experience with aliens but can't because of his skepticism," Sally said. "He always remembers that the little gray man he's about to see is from that book *The Andreasson Affair.*" She let down her faded hair, curled it back up, stuck the four pins in place, and smoothed the top of her head. "He might be the only poet laureate who still reads science fiction."

"The dark secrets," Dickie muttered.

"What did you see?" Sally said to Jenna.

"Frank's teasing me. They were weather balloons."

"I thought for a while," Frank said, "that I was losing my wife to the religion of alienography."

"Don't be silly." Jenna passed the tray of crackers and baba ghanoush to her husband. "I only said that I could understand, in this day and age, why people who want religion, but are disaffected from their own, would choose aliens to be their angels."

"Do you remember," Frank said, "the mom and pop of abductees—Betty and Barney Hill in the early sixties? They seemed perfectly normal, perfectly sane. They had their abduction experience twelve days after they'd seen the 'Bellero Shield' episode of *The Outer Limits*."

Sally said, "I had a patient once who hadn't actually seen a Martian but he was a believer. I said to him, 'Why would they be interested in us? Why would they continue to harvest eggs and sperm, taking the same samples, over and over again? If they are so intellectually superior, which aliens always seem to be, why do they keep repeating the experiments? Don't they have freezers?' "

Frank snorted. "Wasn't it Swedenborg who became a mystic after he'd had temporal-lobe seizures?"

Dickie said, "He spoke with inhabitants on each of the planets in our solar system. He reported that Lunarians speak very loudly from the abdomen."

Jenna thought of the three boys standing in the moonlit field. Three boys "in the grip," Charlie had written, "of an unbearable light." It was difficult to imagine the scene without picturing it as a film—the boys, shoulders thrust back, chests forward, heads tilted upward, mouths open, the light

growing bright, brighter, until it overtakes them, the white-
ness of the ship's beam filling the screen. Jenna hoped that
Charlie's aliens did not resemble any creature from a movie
that had been released shortly before his notable evening.
Surely it would be disappointing when you realized that your
special-occasion encounter was the result of Universal Stu-
dios' production team, when you understood that you hadn't
even come up with your own details.

"There was that crazy Harvard psychologist," Sally said,
"the guy who got on board for abductees, who seemed to
believe them. He said that to listen to one of them talk was
to be in the presence of a truth teller, to be in the presence of
a sacred reality. As I remember it, Harvard ended up investi-
gating his research methods because his conclusions were so
bizarre."

On they talked. The dust glittered in the long afternoon
shafts of light. They talked about the treatment of the Iraqi
translators inside the Green Zone, they talked about the fra-
gility of habeas corpus, and they argued about the most recent
published story by Jenna's writer, the Saint. They all knew
better than to ask Dickie about his own writing, as he never
spoke about it. He laughed when Jenna admitted that, after
interviewing authors for most of her life, she didn't really,
with the exception of the Saint's oeuvre, give a shit anymore
about the creative process. She didn't know why everyone was
so interested in the mystery of creation—let it be! Let it happen without questioning it. When she looked back at her col-

lege classmates, she realized that you could not have predicted who would become the real artists, those who would be disciplined enough to use their talents. Even though she didn't want to hear about their work schedules and where they got their ideas, she hadn't gotten over being surprised by the unlikely people who had burst through with their gifts.

Dickie said that it was true, that even if you thought you'd identified the real writers in a classroom there was often someone ten or twenty years later whom you'd hear on the radio reading his poems while you happened to be driving to the recycling center.

Sally curled up on the swing and napped while they talked about the ouster of an opera singer from the Met, a woman whose contract was not renewed because of her girth. Dickie sang a snippet of a Puccini aria, and wondered what the world was coming to if a diva wasn't allowed to weigh 280 pounds. Although they knew better, they believed on the porch that everyone in the country was held by their same fascinations, that everyone read the same magazines and novels, that the culture had not moved beyond 1955, that their enthusiasms were those of the mainstream. This mirage was a great comfort.

When Frank announced that the meat, which must cook for seven hours, had another two to absorb the spices, to saturate itself with its juices, Jenna wondered if her guests might like to see Prairie Wind Farm. It was, after all, the showplace of Hartley. They could take a walk through the copses, Dickie would remember when he was a shy boy in the wilds of South Dakota, and when they returned it would be a respectable hour, finally, for cocktails. It did occur to Jenna that Charlie might be working, that they might spot him through an arbor arranging the roots of a bush in a deep hole, mending a fence, or he might be standing still, face to the heavens, in a field of poppies. Laura Rider was sure to be there, too, encouraging her customers to buy, to plant, to cultivate, to discover their own artistry.

As Jenna was waiting for Sally to get her purse, she pictured Charlie in her kitchen. Charlie airborne, descending upon them; Charlie suddenly beside her. She and Frank, Dickie, and Sally were all accustomed to accommodating people who did not have their own frames of references. They would draw Charlie out. They would be interested in him as a bit of Hartley sociology, as an artifact. An artifact? A bit of Hartley sociology? Had she drunk too much gin? Why was she inserting Charlie into her party as local color? Why throw him in, even imaginatively, with Sally—Dr. Karmauth—and Dickie, the genius, not to mention the Honorable Judge Voden, author of *Traditions of Law and Jurisprudence*? But surely if Charlie were present he'd perform admirably, or well enough, anyway. In his self-deprecating way he'd defend his UFOs. He'd suggest that the movie executives, the TV producers, and the average citizen had had the same visual experiences at the same time in the early 1960s because the aliens maybe—who could say?—were real. He would wonder if the consciousness hadn't became collective in an instant.

"Are you all right?" Dickie had appeared in the hall and was putting his skinny arms around her. If only Jenna had been attracted to Dickie, she could have run off with him. She loved him best. If she had been interviewing Dickie instead of Frank Voden at the college radio station when she was eighteen, it would perhaps have been the poet who guided her into adulthood. But it wasn't too late! They could escape to a southern climate, leave Sally—who was always caring, and always composed, too—leave her to sing with Frank. It would probably be tedious to be married to someone who had long depressions and occasional affairs, someone who worked so privately, but in the moment, listening to his poet's heart beating, she liked the idea; that is, it made sense to be in love—if she were going to be in love—with someone who wrote so exquisitely and truthfully.

At Prairie Wind Farm they walked aimlessly along the same wooded corridors Charlie had shown Jenna the week before. She had failed to think through the expedition, failed to realize that her friends, quiet people on their own, were inveterate talkers in company, that they would not stop the conversation to appreciate the Riders' accomplishments. The place was as fantastical as before; she had not exaggerated its haunting loveliness to herself or the others. Charlie had sent her a few amusing character sketches of his employees, and she had a new respect for his ability to manage his workers and keep the grounds looking so dewy. When she saw him in the distance by the clapboard farmhouse where he lived, she longed once more for that feeling she'd had with him; it had been as if she were a girl, as if they'd both been released backward to their long-ago selves. Why did she keep returning to that sense of him, and why did such a witless thing seem beautiful? She wondered about the Riders' house, if it was filled with the artful whimsy and simplicity of the gardens, if they had transformed their ordinary Midwestern farmhouse into a dreamscape.

The friends were strolling without purpose, despite Frank's repeating that they should start for home, that the lamb was in grave danger of drying out. The three came along after Jenna with their heads down, discussing whether they should play Scrabble in French.

"You always win in French," Sally was saying to Dickie, "whereas some of us have a chance in English."

"Remember the time we played in German?" Dickie said rapturously.

"Gloating does not become you," his wife said. "And you do it so seldom it always comes as a shock."

Jenna did not want to play Scrabble after dinner in any language. Frank, as always, would work solely for the score, unjustly racking up a huge number of points with easy words; Dickie would conjure his turn out of five vowels and one *j*; Sally would be motherly and praise all efforts; and Jenna, useful only in setting up opportunities so the others could rush in and triumph, would drink more and grow sleepy. She looked about herself, at the planting beyond the path, at the sea of grasses which she thought were bergamot and Culver's root and butterfly weed and senna, among other things that she could not name. It seemed again not enough to look upon the beauty; she wanted, somehow, to splash into it, as if the flowers were water, as if she could run out into the waves of Mrs. Rider's design. She wondered again about their house, and how the couple moved around inside it, husband and wife, co-workers, sometimes friends, and no doubt sometimes enemies. She wondered if she'd ever be able to grasp again that peculiar solace she'd felt before, when she'd walked with Charlie.

When they got home, she went right upstairs to check her e-mail. Vanessa hadn't written or called in two days, which was cause for either celebration or worry. But instead of her daughter there was crider, with a short message:

*Subj: Dream come true?*
*From: crider@kingmail.com*
*To: JFaroli@wis.staff.edu*

*Because I often imagine you walking along the grape arbor I cannot be sure if it was you, or if I was tricking myself. Either way, vision or reality, your presence is a joy to me. Did I see you? Charlie*

"Ridiculous," she said, smiling—she was smiling. "You are ridiculous." She wasn't sure if she was speaking to herself or to Charlie. Sally was starting up her singing again, this time the Italian song in praise of her lover's mouth. *Un bocca bocca bella*, literally "the beautiful mouth mouth," a mouth so glorious you had to repeat the word. That was the first occasion when Jenna thought about Charlie's mouth, the first occasion when she fixed on what she remembered, finding, to her surprise, that she could see it clearly, the fleshy lower lip, and the thinner peaked line above. Her heart didn't lurch, but she did feel an ache, a pull that had old meaning to her, a feeling she'd let go of years before, a feeling, she would have said, that was foolishness, and a sad one at that.

# Chapter 9

LAURA BELIEVED THAT THE BEST PART OF ANY ROMANCE WAS the lead-up, the building of sexual tension even while both parties were uncertain about the feelings of the beloved. She had watched *Pride and Prejudice*, and she had enjoyed her fright as the attraction between Keira Knightley and Matthew Macfadyen, and also the panic, escalated. She happened to like stories where the heroine is in complete shock at the moment when the hero reveals his love: shock, because her own emotions are unknown to her.

Charlie had told Laura his e-mail password, Beaver, the name of their dead dog, and so she had been privy to Jenna's messages. She sometimes wrote back to Jenna, always as Charlie, of course, when he was not around, but more often she composed with him, her laptop on the kitchen table. At first she wished he wasn't writing so much on his own, and she tried, tactfully, to restrain him. "I miss out on the fun when you write to Mrs. Voden without me," she'd say, or "Let's write her another poem. That first one was hilarious." Or, more bluntly, "I'm feeling left out, Chuck." She could see, however, that what was developing between the two of them—or, in actuality, the three of them—was a conversation, and she could understand that when she was busy and away he felt the need to keep it rolling along.

In her abiding fantasy she had always been the star pupil of Jenna, and although it surprised her in the beginning that Jenna continued to write back, in a certain way the teacher's attention felt normal to her. It seemed right. She did on occasion have to remind herself that she was not Laura who was writing, she was Charlie; this did, now and again, take some effort. But one of the unexpected perks of the project so far was the fact that she felt closer to Charlie than she had in a long time, the two of them merged into the single character who was Jenna's pen pal, who was "crider." In this regard they were like Vera Nabokov and her husband, the subjects of a Jenna Faroli program a few years back, spouse and writer working as a team. Mrs. Voden, she and Charlie called Jenna—Mrs. Voden, their joint creation.

It had seemed right, too, that her husband from the start was worshipful of Jenna. He had always been a romantic person, not only about love, but about goodness. If there was any quality that was girlish about him, it was that saccharine drip that ran steadily through his veins; it was a quality that had taken an embarrassingly long time to annoy Laura. She wondered if a person like Jenna would be scornful of Charlie's wide-open spigot, the devotion spraying from him, Charlie the gusher, Charlie the eternal geyser of love. After a few years of courtship, she'd wanted to put a plug in him. If you were vulnerable, as Laura had been in her twenties, you were a goner with that kind of schmaltz, but if you were someone like Jenna, you might, sooner rather than later, register Charlie's fountain of love as nothing more than the penis wagging its tongue.

Not that Charlie—or she and Charlie—were making love through e-mail, or not exactly, not yet. But he'd drawn a portrait of Jenna in ink, without the committee's knowledge or approval, laboring over the picture for a week, apparently, and then he'd scanned it into the computer and sent it to her.

"You drew a portrait?" Laura said at breakfast, when he'd mentioned it so casually, as if she had known all along. "You sent it to her late last night?"

"Yup." Charlie, watching his wife ripping the coated plastic of the coffee bag with her teeth, could tell that she was displeased. "Is that against the law?"

"It's a little pushy." He hadn't, after all, drawn Laura until they'd been together for three months. It was the portrait, for her, that had sealed the deal, how he'd captured what he'd called her heartbreaking tenderness. There was no one more full of shit than Charlie, even if sometimes it was in the nicest possible way, and even though Charlie believed his own bullshit through and through. Over the noise of the coffee grinder Laura said, "If you ever say 'Fucking A' to her again, I'll have to bean you."

"I apologized!" He had to shout to be heard. Why was she bringing up that old mistake? "I told her I was sorry. You— you didn't tell the story about the Silver People the way I wanted you to. You didn't—"

"What?" The short assault of the grinding concluded.

"I said I apologized."

"Did she like it?" his wife asked.

"You know what she said. After I said I was sorry, she wrote me something like 'Dear fucking idiot.'"

"No—did she like the portrait?"

"The portrait?"

"What did she say about it, Charlie?"

"She said it was lovely." That word, the one the girls were crazy about. He stirred his Froot Loops.

"What else?"

"She said she was going to have T-shirts made with the portrait on the front, and sell them on eBay, and also make her staff wear them. She said with the proceeds she and I could run off to St. Barts."

Laura flung open the cupboard and banged it shut.

It was possible to enjoy his wife's wrath, but only if he was just as angry. When they'd fought in the early years, they'd ended up in bed, but now if she was irritated she tended to stay in that mode longer than was any fun, and without the ultimate payoff. He had plenty of reasons to get worked up, to blame her for taking over his story—he could get himself on a roll if given another half a chance—but he thought it probably wasn't worth it. "I'll get the laptop," he said, "and we can write her back."

The minute he set the computer before her at the table, she felt calmness settling through her, as if the screen itself were a drug. Ah, she thought, and Okay, and Here we go. "Dear you," she wrote. It was intimate to be sure, *Dear you.* "Even if you sold T-shirts that only *said* Jenna on them, they'd make millions." There had been, from the start, the question of how much of Charlie someone like Jenna was willing to accommodate. Laura deleted what she'd written. There was not necessarily a delicate balance between slathering it on and being honest, but there was a balance nonetheless. She suddenly felt warmth toward Charlie, toward the goof who used the torch approach when a match was adequate. She turned to her husband. "What do we say?"

"We say, 'Send the T-shirts to press. I would like Jenna Faroli's beautiful puss next to my skin.'"

"Charlie!" She swatted him over the head with a place mat. "You're terrible." She started to laugh. "You're disgusting!"

"I didn't say *pussy.* I said puss. And she knows I'm just kidding." He put his head down and sucked up the pink milk from his cereal bowl.

⌒

After breakfast, Laura had to sit herself at her desk and think the project through again. It did seem as if it was slightly out of control, maybe, but she had meant, after all, for it to go in, or at least toward, this direction. She was realizing that there were a couple of problems with the structure of the relationships. That is, in a traditional romance, the heroine was supposed to be socially, intellectually, and financially inferior to the hero, so that in all areas the love was lifting her up. If Jenna fell for Charlie, it wasn't going to have anything to do with a wish to improve her status, and it might not be about self-improvement, or self-knowledge. If she fell for him, it was going to be pure. The other uncharacteristic part of the situation was Jenna's marriage. Laura could see that it would be easier to fool around with a donkey if you already had a stallion back in the paddock. If the experiment was going to run true, if she was to prove that Jenna could love Charlie in an everyday kind of way, Frank—she laughed out loud— Frank would have to be killed. The book could be a murder mystery and a romance!

But seriously: so many complications. So many difficulties. Laura had wanted to see if someone like Charlie—but wait, there wasn't anyone else like Charlie—to see if Charlie could be made into the man for Jenna. That plan had seemed ingenious at the beginning, but she had failed to understand how she might feel if the romance actually heated up. That possibility had seemed so remote, she hadn't thought to factor her own self into the story. Therefore, the thing was, if it got sexual—say it got sexual—how would she feel about it? Would Charlie cheat on his best girl? The girl he'd sworn to love on earth, in outer space, in all of their incarnations to come, as he had loved her in past lives, including when they'd been prehistoric birds and tadpoles and slime molds? Casting Charlie, for a moment, aside, could Jenna Faroli, deep down under her fully loaded brain, be a vulnerable woman, a woman who was in need of a grand passion? Although any man looked sexy in a judge robe, maybe Frank wasn't the snorting, pawing stallion Jenna all through the years had longed for. If it happened, Laura was sure to know, because Charlie Rider was an open book, because Charlie's eyes would go shiny.

All through the day, as she instructed her work crew, as she waited on customers, and later, when she was back at her desk doing accounts, she turned the burning question over and over: when she found out, how would she feel? The odd thing was, she couldn't tell. She guessed she was removed from the potential pain because of the excitement and the challenges of the project itself. She didn't know if that was good or bad, a mark for or against her. Did it mean she was a terrible person or a committed artist, or both? And another stumper: when Laura was not taking Jenna's messages for granted, when she really thought about it, she was amazed by how easily Jenna had gotten caught up in the correspondence. That Jenna wanted to communicate with Laura/Charlie was definitely a boost to Laura's self-esteem. But it was weird, too, that Jenna was wasting her time on Charlie, that she'd write him so contemplatively, that she'd bring up philosophical matters. On the other hand, she could be enigmatically brief. After she'd come to the farm with her friends, she had written to Charlie, "I saw you."

*I saw you.* Was the line charged? You had to wonder. Or was Laura reading too much into the sentence? The fact was that, so far, the radio personality was a mystery. What Laura had to remember was that Jenna Faroli was her subject. Studying Jenna was the goal. She must keep in mind that if Jenna, the most superior kind of woman, could love Charlie, then Every Woman was capable of loving him, and Laura would understand the universal female. Laura must always keep her eye on that prize. The tables could very well be turned in her romance, the woman, by her love, raising up the man to his fullest potential. Maybe her very own Charlie Rider was the man for the twenty-first century, a new model. A male who was not the slacker type, not a slob on a sofa making crass jokes but a man who was serious. A man in earnest about being submissive by day and a conqueror by night. A man who, when he went to war, would make the enemy laugh, a man who tried to become one with the chipmunks, a man who was at home in the universe, a man who loved his own sperm—one million and one, one million and two—because they were such good swimmers, and because nearly all of them died for nothing.

"You should arrange to meet Mrs. Voden for coffee," Laura said to her husband the next morning. "Ask her how her garden is doing. You could offer to go over there and take a look."

Charlie had the good fortune to have supple skin that did not go leathery in summer. He was looking well, she thought, not only because he was fit and bronzed, but because his eyes were going into the love mode. It was as if the love were a liquid that was filling him up to the eyeballs. So it was happening. She made a mental note to make a real note: Charlie, wet eyes, barometer of love. It hit her then, that this was it. Right here and now, this was it in real, actual life. Charlie was leaving her. Not physically, no, but in the other equally important ways, emotionally, spiritually, psychically. "Charlie," she called softly. She put her head down on the table and stretched one hand across to his place. She wanted to tell him not to go too far, not to go beyond the garden gate. "Charlie!"

He was at the sink, running the water, filling the coffeepot, knowing, without hearing the sense of her murmurs, that she was discussing a topic of great importance with the two cats who were sacked out at her feet.

The third meeting of Mrs. Voden and Charlie a few days later, as told to Laura by her husband, went on longer than he'd figured. They had coffee at the one café in Hartley, called the Queen Bee. "I talked too much," Charlie reported to his wife.

"What did you tell her?"

"About Mom and Dad-o. About—"

"Drinking out of the bottle until you were seven?"

"The whole story."

Women, Laura considered, would like that detail, the idea of little Charlie having breastlike comfort, and the idea that Charlie's mother had been relaxed and loving enough to ignore the child-rearing experts. "Did you tell her about barely graduating from high school?"

"Like I said, I told her everything."

Had that been smart? If Jenna liked Charlie enough, she would appreciate how intuitive he was even though people in Hartley thought he was at heart a loser and a fruitcake. But if Jenna was just passing the time with Charlie, for her own bizarre reasons, if she was having a conversational fling, she would probably think that Charlie was, in fact, a loser. Still, Jenna had experience with all kinds of people, and Laura's guess was that she would be impressed by Charlie's ability to make something of himself even if his high-school teachers hadn't been able to get him to read the assigned books or do his written homework.

Since the morning when Charlie's eyes had been doing the telltale glistening, Laura had given herself many stern talkings-to, reminding herself that this, after all, was her plan, and reassuring herself, too, that she was pretty much in charge, more or less, because of her access to the e-mails. She wouldn't let Charlie stray very far, and in the meantime she was going to learn so much from the experiment, the adventure, the gamble—the whatever it was.

"What do you think Jenna likes about you?" Laura said.

Charlie drummed his fingers on the kitchen table. "Is this Twenty Questions?"

"Maybe."

"She likes me because, even though I'm scrawny, I'm a stud. She likes me because she has never met anyone as studly as myself."

"But besides that. Why else?"

"Okay, okay." He rested his head on his fists and thought awhile. "She likes me because she knows she's not going to have to interview me about nuclear physics or international labor laws. She's not going to have to keep—whatever they're called—the Sunnis and the Shiites straight."

"She likes you because you don't know about anything important?"

"Bingo."

"You're restful to be with?"

"Restful, that's it. Restful."

Everything he'd told his wife was true. There were, however, several details that Charlie had omitted in the story of his date with Jenna. They had not spent time in the café but instead had ordered their coffee and morning buns to go. He had told her he'd like to show her a favorite spot in a county park, about six miles south of Hartley. They had driven in his car through town, past the ice-cream shop, the bait shop, the resale shop, and the therapist's house, which was also her office. He told her about the therapist, Sylvia Marino, about Sylvia's troubles with her fifteen-year-old daughter. Every afternoon, the girl sat on the steps of her house—also the steps of the therapy office—with five boys, five lugs, who were her only friends, and seemed to be vying for her affections. Ariana Marino splayed herself across the steps, and the five enormous boys surrounded her, leaden moons to her gaseous planet. Periodically Sylvia would come out and shoo them away, but the next day there they were again, sprawled on the stairs. All the people who were in counseling had to step over them to get to their appointments. Jenna had loved that story, and he'd driven them around the block twice, looking for any sign of fair Ariana.

Once they got to the park, they walked along the path through the restored prairie, and along the crest of a hill where there was a single tree, a stocky burr oak with generous lower limbs. Charlie scrambled up to the spot he used to come to after his grandfather died. He reached down to Jenna and helped her to sit beside him. She seemed unconcerned about getting her light linen pants dirty, a quality he admired in a woman. "How I love a pretty little girl," he sang in his gravelly voice, "Lord only knows. She brought me a letter, and said she'd be mine, and I can hardly wait to love her all the time."

The trees were well past the delicacy of their leafing and into the full-bodied vigor of summer. How beautiful and strong the world was! How free Charlie and Jenna were, alone, away from everyone who loved them. "Sometimes," he said to her, "I think of telling you secrets."

She was gazing out to a pond in the distance.

Jane Hamilton

"Sometimes I'd like to tell you that my wife won't, you know, sleep with me. That she gave it up years ago. I'd like to tell you that this seems unfair . . ." Jenna was very still. She didn't turn her head or make a sound or appear to be listening. "It makes me," he whispered, "sad."

"I know" was all she said, after a minute.

She didn't tell him, not until several days later, in a message, what she'd been thinking. In the moment she could feel herself swimming in the cool water of the pond that was down the hill and past the cornfield. She was swimming in that imaginary girlhood, a childhood that had unfolded with Charlie, a long-ago life together. She could see it and hear it, the details, the plinth of their bond, a secret language, a place in the crook of a tree with chipped teacups, the escape at night through an old lake house, through the wet grass, to swim naked in the black water. It was that idea, up in the tree, perhaps more than the man himself that made her reach for him. There, the first kiss! He clasped her face—and between them there were astonished and grateful smiles. He kissed her cheeks, her brow, and then the second kiss, longer than the first, and deeper. Charlie did not think of Mrs. Rider much. How could he when he had Jenna in his arms, Jenna with her creased white eyelids solemnly shut and her tongue so shyly exploratory. Because he had always been prone to think in ecclesiastical terms when it came to love, he believed that he was nearing heaven's gate, that he was about to be welcomed, after the long absence, back to paradise.

# Chapter 10

ON A SCORCHING DAY AT THE END OF JUNE, JENNA WAS sitting in Studio B, just finished with the morning's program, a show that had featured three authors of Hillary books, all of them patched in from around the country. The studio was dim in the corners and cool, and Jenna, by herself, felt miles from stalled traffic and fierce sunlight and the gang shooting that had occurred not far from the station at dawn, and presidential candidates, including Hillary, who in unlikely small towns were recovering from their pancake breakfasts and preparing for their picnics. She would have to get out in a minute, making way for David Oberhaus, who did the daily read-aloud show, but she liked sitting in the stillness, with her mike in front of her, the sleek cylinder that felt as if it were part of her, an extension of her vocal cords. Suzie Raditz had once told Jenna that in the post-show moments she could see

Jenna's on-air self—that large, generous, unfailingly curious character—get coiled up and put away, stored for another day's use. Jenna had supposed it was an insult, and yet there was probably truth in it. The outsized on-air Jenna was not necessary back in the office preparing for yet another show.

She could see Suzie through the window, at the control desk, talking to Pete Warner, the engineer. Gone were Suzie's frumpy drawstring pants and plain T-shirts and worn-out sandals. She was wearing a summer dress, a yellow sleeveless frock that was not inappropriate, not really, and yet she walked with a self-conscious boldness, and she stood with defiance, her arms crossed under her breasts, her feet, in dainty heels, planted wide. It was her impenitence that seemed lewd. Jenna understood that there is no one as wildly happy as the middle-aged woman who has discovered or rediscovered her sexual self. She had seen the type countless times. There is perhaps no one as self-absorbed or as careless even as she takes pains to go in secret. Suzie, despite the new dress, however, did not look radiant or youthful or exhilarated. Her skin was gray, she had circles under her eyes, and the concealer she wore on her neck drew attention to the hickeys rather than masking them. It had been years since Jenna had seen a hickey. Had they gone out of fashion? Or was Jenna not around enough young people? She should ask Suzie if hickeys were making a comeback in the culture at large.

It did not surprise her that as soon as she sat down at her desk Suzie was at her office door. She had felt the Raditz, as

Pete Warner called her, coming on as one feels a headache or a bad cold gathering force. The weight loss had made the producer's long nose seem longer, and her green eyes larger and closer together. Love, it seemed, was a starvation diet.

"It's interesting," Suzie said, "that, no matter how well re-searched those Hillary books are, no matter how much time the author has spent following her around, you never really get a sense of who she is." She closed the door and sat across the desk from Jenna.

That morning, Pete had also barged into Jenna's office, in order to deliver an oration on Suzie's breasts, in order to hold forth about how the technologically advanced brassiere he believed she now wore, an undergarment that was intended to lift and separate, did not fit Suzie, and that, although her boobies were higher than their naturally sucked-out mother-tit selves, they also looked squashed, cramped, unnatural, and dangerous. The threat level of her breasts, he'd explained to Jenna, was ORANGE.

"Thank you, Pete," Jenna had said.

Suzie plucked a tissue from the box on the desk—a bad sign, Jenna knew. "I need your help," Suzie said, dabbing at her nose. "I really need your assistance. I'm in over my head, Jenna."

"What seems to be the problem?" Jenna was trying not to look at Suzie's chest, trying not to remember what Pete had said about the threat level.

"Let me just say that I know it's not exactly fair to bring

issues like this to you. I know that. You've always been clear about the boundaries. But you're the only person who can help, the only one who can go—"

"What's the matter?"

"The matter is . . . the matter is David Oberhaus."

"David?" The professor of English who'd done the read-aloud half-hour segment at twelve-fifteen for as long as Suzie had been at the station.

"I've been having a—a thing with David, a thing—"

"Suzie." Jenna tried to modulate her voice so that there was an undertone of warmth, a very quiet undertone, barely detectable, but present. She did not want to sound unfeeling, but she had no intention of encouraging Suzie, of falling down the black hole of need that was Suzie Raditz. "I can tell you're distressed," Jenna said. "You look exhausted. Do you need a few days off? A week? Or two?"

"I need your help. Please, Jenna. You were so great to me when my mother was sick. You were there for me, and I've never forgotten it, I haven't. It's just that I need that kind of support again."

Jenna had made the error, early on in Suzie's tenure. She had been young, too, and hadn't yet understood that her staff could not be her friends. After the mother had died and Suzie had regained her strength, Jenna drew back, declining her dinner invitations and outings to the movies, and avoiding the heart-to-hearts. They had gone on together in what Jenna hoped was a rewarding working relationship for Suzie.

"I'm worried," Suzie was saying, "about David. I mean seriously worried. And if this thing gets out, and it looks like it might—"

"I can give you time off. Go away with your husband. Take the kids to the Dells. Get yourself rested and grounded—"

"You're not hearing me." She was crying now, pulling tissue after tissue out of the box. "I need you to talk to people in Administration. I need you to go to David, to make sure he doesn't—"

"I am hearing you, Suzie." Jenna spoke evenly. Pushing the tissue box closer to her employee was the best show of support she could manage. "I'm not available to help you cover up your adultery. I hope that's clear. The less I know, actually, the better. I'm not going to talk to Gary, I'm not going to discuss it with David. It's none of my business."

"I'm trying to talk to you," Suzie pleaded, "as a friend. Is that too much to ask? I've worked for you for sixteen years. I've always been—"

"Invaluable," Jenna said, standing up. "But that doesn't mean I'm going to get involved with your scandal. If you need time off, let me know." She went to the door and put her hand on the knob. "Try to find the thrill in sound judgment." She paused, to let that idea sink in. "I'd prefer not to lose you. That would be terrible. You know how much I depend on your curiosity, your ability to probe a subject, and your gift for making connections. You know I couldn't operate as I do without you. However, this is simple office decorum. You understand the rule, that you don't shit where you eat. I hope you can keep whatever situation you've gotten into under control." In the moment, she had the small satisfaction of not having capitulated. "I know you'll work it out." She left Suzie sobbing, soaking the eyelet lap of her yellow sundress.

~~~~~

Shortly after Suzie's crisis, Jenna was making her way home from her first county-park assignation with Charlie. Frank was always in the backdrop of her mind, but she wasn't actively thinking about him, and neither did she dwell on the three ticks that had come crawling down her arm, which she sliced to pieces with her fingernail. She tried not to think about more burrowing into her back and her scalp, tried not to think about the complications of Lyme disease. Instead, she pictured Ariana, the therapist's daughter in Hartley, who spent her afternoons with her suitors on the steps of her mother's office. How would the princess choose just one boy? She thought, too, of Suzie Raditz and David Oberhaus. What had Jenna said to Suzie? *Try to find the thrill in sound judgment.* What fly-by-night Girl Scout leader had that come from? David was genial, had a soft, feminine-looking mouth, and was an Americanist, specializing in Faulkner, Hemingway, Fitzgerald, Dos Passos, Robert Penn Warren. Suzie's husband was not so different from David physically, but he was an entomologist for the county extension. Had Suzie wanted someone she could talk to about books, or was David's appeal unrelated to his love for the big cats of American literature? Whatever the attraction, Jenna imagined that Suzie had filled her dresser with black lace crotchless panties, that she'd hidden them under her extra-large T-shirts, which she wore as pajamas in her tired marriage to the bug man.

Jenna's biggest fear, as she drove home, in fact, was becoming someone who was even remotely like Suzie Raditz. If that should happen, she'd have to ask Pete Warner to shoot her. She wondered if the people of Hartley had seen her with Charlie: the people of Hartley in a straight line, including the garden-club ladies, and the Greek man who owned the Queen Bee Café, and Ariana and her beaux, and the postmistress—all of them advancing together up the hill to spy on Jenna Faroli of the *Jenna Faroli Show*. She thought of Pete, her one true ally at the station, one of the few people who did not want her job. She knew that if Pete were part of the Hartley Battalion he would think less of her; he might even feel betrayed. Enormous, bearded Pete, who was devoted to Jenna, who hadn't had a girlfriend in a decade, who was a ham-radio and news junkie, who ate every single meal at Subway. It was the two of them who stood above the foolishness of the mortals at the station. It was Pete who, if he caught sight of Charlie, would say, "Him? You can't be serious—that clown?" She could not imagine what Frank might think or say. It was far easier to conjure Pete, incredulous Pete.

She had had the privilege of meeting—of flirting, even—with remarkable men. Although hormone therapy had failed to supply her with heat and moisture, she now and again had a guest on the show who she suspected could do the job. But those people were not real possibilities. She had no interest in a long-distance affair, and she would never create a mess Suzie Raditz–style at the station. Frank and Vanessa and her work were plenty of happiness; they were, in fact, an embarrassment of riches.

She was relieved, after her expedition with Charlie, that Frank was not at home. She went out into the yard to look at the delphiniums, the spires of blue and purple and white blooms that, since she'd staked them, stood tall and straight, as if with rectitude. She had not considered how dangerous music could still be at her age, and certainly she had never feared the twangy songs of the mountains. And yet Charlie singing to her had been far more effective than hormone therapy, far more effective than her recent conversations in the studio with Robert Redford or Sting or the host of handsome legends who trooped in. She and Charlie had come down from the tree and had lain in the tick-infested grass for the better part of an hour, with all the sweetness and wonder of first love, and also the stirrings of mature and urgent lust. What strong force had held back the floodwaters, what steel gate had kept them at bay for so many years? In the arms of Charlie Rider the dike had broken. She had arched her back—*arched her back*!

Charlie, in response, had whispered, "Love, do you want to see . . . it?"

She had said she'd rather not. That is, she wanted to see it, of course she did, but not quite yet.

"Not that it's anything spectacular," he said. "I didn't mean it was extra-special, I was only, you know, offering."

"I want," she said breathlessly, "to have a little more time to imagine it." Was there any clearer invitation, any clearer signal than the arched back?

He had placed his hand at her lumbar, and she'd lowered down into his firm palm, the smallest gesture that suggested he could hold all of her. She had not been able to stop trembling.

At home, she went inside into the refurbished master bathroom—a long, narrow, empty room, with a white-tiled floor, a chandelier, and a tub on claws by the window. She took off her grass-stained linen pants and ran the water until it was scalding. In the bath, she examined her dimpled legs and the pudding of her stomach with a newly critical and dismayed eye. She cried out. She wished to be beautiful, and it was impossible. She could see that if she fell into this *thing*—as Suzie had called adultery—she would be filled with longing for what she could not be and have. She would yearn for Charlie, she would want him to write her several times a day, to call her, to come to her window. She would not mind if he took risks to see her, provided it turned out well. When he didn't oblige her, she would be racked with sorrow. And she might now and again have clarity, as piercing as a blade to the heart, the passing understanding of her bad judgment. She would be as tormented as she was happy. She could also see far ahead, and so she knew that when she came out of the spell, after the potion had worn off, she would be left with only the deepest regret.

⌒

Three days later, they met again in the county park, this time at dusk. He spread a brown army blanket on a small clear space they'd found in a thicket. The evening was windy—an important bit of luck, because the breeze had carried off most of the mosquitoes. He dropped his shorts to the ground and up it sprang: Hello! Hello! It was a violent purple with one glistening drop at the tip. She had forgotten the splendor of eagerness, and she could do nothing but kneel before it, stroking it as if it were a soft midsized animal, kissing it, patting it on the head, before she brought its velvetiness to her mouth. When he begged her to stop, in order to pace himself, she did so reluctantly.

"Now you," he said.

Together they got her out of her hemp pants. "Oh my God," Charlie said, covering his mouth. He, a more or less perfect specimen, save for a rash on his back, seemed to be stricken by the loveliness of her body, by the indoor white lumpishness of her flesh; stricken by the welt of her scar, the rude reminder of her hysterectomy, stricken by her broad hips, her thinning pubic hair, and her ample bottom. She did ask herself, in the briefest moment of reason, how she had come to be lying on a scratchy blanket, naked, and probably resembling a small harpoonable whale. And yet she felt like an ingénue. The breeze on her skin was wonderful, and there was the smell of him, an endearing mix of cinnamon and baby powder and citrus. "Impale me," she heard herself say.

"You are so beautiful," he murmured.

What miracle had Charlie wrought? What miracle was he? Had she actually said, *Impale me*? Had she actually said to Suzie Raditz, *Try to find the thrill in sound judgment*? She would burn in hell for her hard, cold treatment of Suzie but she wasn't going to—couldn't—think about it now. Nothing mattered, nothing, except that she and Charlie were together in this unwinding of years. Backward they went as she arched again and he kissed her breasts, and then, while she held her strong thighs aloft, her buttocks lifted in what he guessed must be a yoga pose, he deftly secured the condom, tweaking the tip, and opening his eyes wide. "I love you," he pronounced. Slowly he drove himself into the core of her.

A few minutes later, it was not the memory of her aunt's china tea service or a plated runcible spoon that gave Jenna the most hallowed sense of the passing of the ages and generations, but herself on all fours, Charlie behind her on his knees, holding her hips and thrusting to a point of exquisite pain. Great-grandmothers, grandmothers, mother, Jenna, daughter, granddaughters, great-granddaughters, and on into the infinity of the future and looping around to the beginning of the world—how she hoped that all of them had been and were and would be fucked exactly, oh God yes, yes, like this.

How could she have forgotten the happiness born from such an unlikely thing? "'I can live no longer by thinking,'" she said out loud in her car, on the way home.

⁓

It is perhaps not surprising that, after that simple, unlikely action, the message situation in the Rider household became somewhat confused. Charlie had told Jenna as they said their fond goodbyes in the county park that she should write her heartfelt messages, if she had them, to a new e-mail address, to CSRider. He had never deliberately lied to his wife, but it was necessary now to hide the more ardent communications in order to protect Laura's feelings. Although he had sensed a motive in her insistence on his friendship with Jenna, he doubted at first that sex had been his wife's plan. She had, he thought, wanted him to get out more, to expand his horizons, to live up to his social potential. But as time passed, he came to think it was possible that Laura, understanding what was missing in his life, was offering him this specific remedy. Laura the matchmaker; Laura, choosing a person for him whom they could both, in different ways, enjoy, and also someone who was not, most likely, going to upset herself or her own marriage over Charlie. Maybe Laura was allowing him Jenna as a way to diffuse her own guilt for not sleeping with him. Where was the therapist, Sylvia Marino, when he needed her? Each idea that came to him seemed equally outlandish and equally plausible. Certainly he had seen Jenna as an opportunity, one he could not refuse. Your wife hands you a lover on a platter and you're going to say no? He'd never had a woman like Jenna, a woman who was so much—a woman. So wonderfully big and soft, someone you could plunge into, a great bowl of dough. Still, whatever Laura was thinking, he did not want to hurt her, and a new e-mail account seemed like protection for all of them.

Laura, naturally, was still writing her own messages to Jenna. They were as loving and heartfelt as Charlie's loving and heartfelt communications. And so Jenna, naturally, often wrote responding to her, as full of feeling to crider as CSRider. What's in a name? What's in an address? When Charlie wrote to Jenna as CSRider about how gentle she was, about how her gentleness was the support for all her strengths, Jenna later wrote back on that topic to crider.

*Subj: Calibrated exquisitely*
*From: JFaroli@wis.staff.edu*
*To: crider@kingmail.com*

*Dearest,*

*You have said that you were teased all your life for being a sissy, but it is your great strength to have both masculine and feminine aspects, the levels calibrated exquisitely. You have none of the bravado of the He-man, and none of the bitch of the She-woman, and yet you have a great store of tenderness—a quality we think of as feminine. All of this is within the you that is fiercely male. Thank you for writing to say that it is gentleness which is*

*my scaffolding, gentleness which holds me up. I shall have
to tell my producer this, as she believes I am without
feeling.*

Laura puzzled over this message. She didn't recall Charlie's
writing to Jenna about her gentleness being her scaffolding,
but it was a powerful statement. She had to hand it to him.
Maybe Laura had overlooked it, a single message among hundreds. She had loved the recent one where Jenna explained
that she felt as if she were a girl in a distant childhood with
Charlie, that somehow they had been young together. It had
been a time, Jenna wrote, when she was young and easy under
the apple boughs, about the lilting house, and happy as the
grass was green. That had been so beautiful. It had choked
her up.

Could it be that Charlie, in order to be loved by Jenna, did
not need a makeover? Did Charlie need no improvement?
Was he, in fact, the ideal hero? Did Jenna bring those heroic
traits out in him, or had Laura forgotten that Charlie was
special, that he was calibrated exquisitely? Or was this it: was
Jenna as screwy as Charlie? *Calibrated exquisitely!* Was Jenna
falling in love? Was Jenna therefore insensible to Charlie's
glaring faults?

They were folding laundry one night, and Laura said,
as if to make idle conversation, "How's it going with Mrs.
Voden?"

"You know how it's going," Charlie said.

"Do I?"

"You read the messages. You *write* the messages, for Christ's sake!"

It was true, of course. An hour before, Laura had told Jenna that she loved her:

Subj: Re: No subject
From: crider@kingmail.com
To: JFaroli@wis.staff.edu

Darling Jenna,
   I often just want to tell you and tell you again and yet again, that I love you, and that there are many reasons why I love you. I love the things you teach me. I have considered you my teacher for so many years, and now there is this new time, where you are before me in person, teaching me more than I thought possible. I love you, C.

Although Laura did not know for certain if they'd had sex, surely it was safe to say that Jenna was teaching Charlie many, many new things in the hours when he was away in parts unknown with Mrs. Voden. "I know I write the messages, some of them," she said, laying out sock after sock on the sofa, "but I'm not the one meeting her for coffee—or whatever."

Charlie finished the undershirt, two sleeves under, folding up the front, the way his wife had taught him, even though he didn't care if his shirts were in a wad in his drawer. He put his arms around her and said, "You were right about Jenna.

You are always right. She is a lovely friend, just like you told me she would be."

There were moments, such as this one, when Laura almost thought she could fall in love with Charlie again. She rested her ear against his mouth.

"What Jenna doesn't know," Charlie whispered, "is that she loves not only me, but you, too. She probably loves me only for the you that is in the messages."

And then they both gingerly lowered themselves to the sofa, so as not to disturb the laundry. They were laughing softly. Laura laughed at the idea that she was falling in love with the writer, Charlie, who was actually, in large measure, herself. She laughed harder. They were all insane! Charlie laughed because Jenna might love the messages but even more she loved how he took her from behind, she loved his endurance, she loved, she said, how in their motel sessions it was as if he was making up a symphony on the spot. He laughed because he and Jenna had been children together in a past life, growing up to screw their Victorian brains out. And so, for their own reasons, the Riders laughed together on the sofa until they wept.

# Chapter 11

THROUGH THE SUMMER, THE LOVEBIRDS MET AT A MOTEL
thirty miles north of Hartley on Saturday afternoons, and
sometimes on Wednesday evenings, too. Frank, as Jenna had
foreseen, had disappeared into the world of jurisprudence,
writing the book that would be of interest to seven legal
scholars, a book that would be intelligent and important
and unread. Jenna herself would fall into a deep sleep while
reading the introduction. Even Dickie would not read it in
its entirety, although he'd have incisive comments and want
to discuss. The writing took Frank to his office whether or
not he was at work in the court, and he often stayed late
in order to crank out another few paragraphs. This allowed
Jenna the liberty to travel to the motel, the Kewaskum Inn,
when she pleased. The Native American–themed rooms had
dream catchers in every window, Indian corn tied with rib-

bon hanging on the bathroom doors, paintings of chiefs in headdresses, snowshoes fashioned out of twigs nailed to the walls, and lampshades made of faux birch bark. The TV remote was bolted to the end table. "I wonder why the injins don't trust the white man," Charlie said.

They would first rip the waxy bedspread from the mattress, and they might then sit primly like shy teenagers or crawl under the covers fully clothed, thereby making the struggle to undress somewhat violent, or they might hurtle themselves at each other, no holds to their passion. She couldn't always recall the sequence, how they found themselves on the floor, or over by the bureau, how it was they got themselves back in bed. Afterward, Jenna, resting her head on Charlie's firm, tanned chest, liked to ask about Mrs. Rider. She was curious about the woman who must be an entrepreneurial as well as artistic genius, not only to have dreamed up Prairie Wind Farm but to have made it a reality. Laura was in one minute wearing steel-toed boots and overalls, shoveling a bed of stones, and in the next going to a bluegrass festival wearing a gauzy blouse and a Prada skirt. It had been purchased, Charlie was quick to explain, on sale. He carried the photograph of his wife in that skirt tucked into his wallet, and Jenna, more than once in her postcoital repose, had asked to see it. Mrs. Rider in that small skirt looked indecent, but sweetly so.

"What's your wife doing today?" Jenna often asked, after the first round.

Charlie, running his fingers up her arm, to her neck, and

smoothing her hair, would say, "Running the world. Overseeing the planet. I love your calmness."

"I'm not calm." Still, she had lowered her voice so that it might sound even more like that of a serene person. "Sometimes," she murmured, "I go into the resale shop in Hartley to buy a silly thing for my daughter, or a sweatshirt or jacket for myself, and I wonder if I'm buying an item that belonged to your wife. We're different sizes, as you can see, but it gives me a strange feeling to imagine that I might take home a sweater that she once wore."

Charlie kissed the top of her head. "She does take her clothes there," he said, "to sell on consignment."

Jenna raised up on her elbow to look at him. "Where does she think you are today? What does she think we're doing?"

"Taking a walk in the woods."

"An extremely long walk. We'll be so tired!"

"Maybe we're training for a marathon."

"A triathlon, I think it is. So many different talents at work here." She nuzzled his clavicle and his ruby-colored nipples. His penis lay flopped to the side of his leg like a tired dog's tongue out the side of the mouth. I am the tired dog, she thought, and Charlie's penis is my tongue. She thought, I'm losing my mind. She wondered, What will become of me? "Why," she said, returning to his shoulder and shutting her eyes, "does she let you go, when there is so much to be done?"

Jenna's phone, across the room on the bureau, sounded in

the ringtone of Mozart's Symphony No. 34 in C Major, K. 338. She buried her face in his neck. "Vanessa," she whimpered.

"She needs you," Charlie said.

Jenna heaved herself out of bed and tiptoed on the sticky carpet to the phone. "Hello, sweetheart," she said, gathering with one hand the spare blanket that had been on the bed and draping herself with it as she settled into the wigwam print of the upholstered chair. "I'm not at home. I'm at the grocery store." She rolled her eyes at Charlie. He opened the end-table drawer and took out the Holy Bible. He held up the book and mouthed, "It's not bolted down!"

Periodically Jenna interjected. "Oh!" And "Did you talk to him?" And "Maybe you could ask for a meeting." And "Did you sleep last night?"

There was very little that made Charlie happier than sexual intercourse. Long ago, Laura, when she had also liked sex, had told him that he'd been born for that single activity, that it was what he could do best. He had considered this a compliment, although he had since thought that maybe it was a put-down. Jenna had not only given him his greatest pleasure back, she had restored his confidence. Here was something he could not fuck up: he could not fuck up fucking.

"Honey, honey, listen," Jenna was saying, "I feel a little strange talking here in the middle of the produce aisle. Can I call you later tonight?" A long silence. "I know you are, I know it. What did the therapist say?"

Charlie read random passages in the Song of Solomon. "Your navel *is* a rounded goblet; it lacks no blended beverage." Rum and coke, he thought, gin and tonic, Jenna and Faroli. "Your waist *is* a heap of wheat set about with lilies." He loved the sound of a heap of wheat but Jenna probably wouldn't find that very flattering. "Your two breasts are like two fawns, twins of a gazelle." Her breasts, if you were going to go the animal route, were more like young and very still rabbits. He already knew that when Jenna asked the therapist question she was going to be on the phone for another fifteen minutes. It didn't matter to him how long she spoke to her daughter. When she came back to bed, she'd be hot and bothered and he would be ready, again, to take her mind off her troubles. He would tell her that her navel lacked no blended beverage, and even though he believed the poet had taken liberties, he also knew it was absolutely true.

A few days later, in the same room, after much the same routine—although it was always different; there was always a way he moved, or a position he wrapped her into, that astonished her—after that, when she was recovering in his arms, she had, not an idea, but an impulse. "Charlie," she said, sitting up. "I'd like to do something for her."

"Who?"

"Mrs. Rider. I'd have you, but that would be complicated and nerve-racking and wrong—if you know what I mean. But I could invite her in for a gardening segment."

Later, of course, she could not believe herself, could not believe she had made the unprofessional, the shameful, the baleful suggestion. She had an ironclad rule that she never asked her friends on the program, not counting Dickie, who had done two shows during his tenure as poet laureate. She would have asked the poet laureate even if he hadn't been Dickie, was her defense.

"Laura?" Charlie yanked himself up. "Is that what you're saying?" With both hands he pushed his curls off his forehead. "Laura on the *Jenna Faroli Show*?"

Jenna, perhaps not incidentally, had never, before that afternoon, had someone bring her to orgasm orally. "It's one little thing I could do for you," she said, "for the farm, for the business. More people need to know about the place. We do this kind of show now and again. We had Stephanie Anderson in the spring talking about garden style. I'll admit it was fun because people called in trashing Martha Stewart, and Stephanie was queenly, as you might imagine, taking the high road, praising Martha for raising the consciousness of gardeners. We, in the studio, could tell how delighted Stephanie was, how gleeful."

"Laura on the show?" Charlie said again.

"Your wife spoke well at the garden-club meeting in Hartley." Jenna was trying to remember if that was true. Laura had seemed quite nervous, but her presentation had been straightforward, and she'd answered the questions without too much hesitation. This was such a small thing—fifteen minutes—that Jenna could do for the Riders.

"In August," Jenna said to Charlie. "It wouldn't be a typical end-of-the-season-type garden show, but something more whimsical, a segment about the names of flowers, or maybe a piece that dealt with the philosophical or, or spiritual tensions when brute labor is required to make a place of beauty, the—"

"I don't think there is anything that would make Mrs. Rider more thrilled," Charlie said, staring at the ceiling, "than being on the *Jenna Faroli Show.*" He was beginning to see the plan: it was occurring to him that getting on Jenna's show had been Laura's goal in this friendship thing all along. She had known that if Charlie did his amazing penis tricks with Jenna she would invite Laura on the program. He knew he was married to a force, but he had not realized just how Machiavellian she was.

"Are you all right?" Jenna said.

"I'm stunned," Charlie said, "that you would do this for her, for us. That you would have her on the show." Should he feel used? Or should he celebrate his wife, a woman who had developed a win-win strategy? Charlie was happy using his greatest gift, and Laura got a giant kickback. So good! He should be happy—he was happy!

"Don't tell her yet," Jenna said. "I've got to map out the program, check to see if it fits in the schedule. Please don't mention it quite yet."

Laura would go ape when he told her. "I understand," he said to Jenna. Could he keep the secret? "Not a word," he muttered, nodding his head solemnly.

⟋⟍

Jenna did not tell anyone about the affair. Dickie was the only friend she might have confided in, but she wanted to talk to him in person. Surely he would be amused by the story, and he'd have a generous spin on her taking up with someone like Charlie, reminding her that she was only human, falling for a longshoreman, the milkman, the party-event clown. He'd bring up Edith Wharton's love for Morton Fullerton, Proust's obsession with his prostitute, Helen Schlegel's coupling with Leonard Bast, and Lady Chatterley's delight in her gamekeeper. Dickie himself, she knew, had had several transgressions, as one might expect of a poet laureate.

She was as careful as she could be, wearing a gray silk scarf and sunglasses, parking in the rear of the Kewaskum Inn, dashing, with as few steps as she could manage, between vehicle and door, into the deluxe dream catcher room—Jacuzzi, king bed, and wireless!—where Charlie, if all went according to plan, would be sprawled across the comforter, as naughty and inviting as a pinup model. When it came time to leave, she peered between the smallest parting of the curtains, to make certain no one, 90.4 FM listener or otherwise, was on the pavement. It did occur to her that the scarf and glasses fairly screamed ADULTERY, but she could not bring herself

to drive to the motel and onto the premises without her fla-
grant disguise.

"Please don't get caught," she urged Charlie. "Please, let's
never get found out."

Once, when she was leaving home on a humid Saturday
afternoon, she locked herself out of the house and found, to
her dismay, that she didn't have her car keys, either. It was
one of those days when she could hardly wait to get to him,
when, if she was going to be reckless, it would be worth it for
that moment, kneeling on the spongy mattress, face to face,
fingers light and kisses deep, the holy time—go slowly, hurry,
go slowly, hurry—before the deeper religious experience. But
she was sitting in her hot car with no keys. She could not
get back into her house. The sweat was soaking her clothes,
and she was smeared into her seat. "Think!" she demanded.
"Think!"

She remembered that one of her study windows did not
have a screen on it, and that it was not locked. If she could
get up to it, she could open it from the outside, and climb
through. In the barn she found an eighteen-foot ladder that
Frank had bought to clean out the eaves troughs, something
in the end he had hired the neighbor to do. The ladder was
aluminum and not terribly heavy, although it was unwieldy.
Jenna managed to get it over to the house and, using all
her strength, she was able to set it by her window. She had
weights that she now and again made a halfhearted attempt
to lift, but that was the extent of her exercise regimen. Setting

the ladder had made her dizzy, and now she must climb, rung by rung, up and up and up. This was how she was going to die. She tried to focus as she had never done before, step, breathe, lift the foot, don't look anywhere but hand and ridged rung. Don't see the rosebushes underneath you, don't dwell on the thick orange thorns which occur at murderously regular intervals along the stem wood. She would fall to her death because she could not get to her lover. Frank would come home and find her splattered parts speared through by the roses. Women were idiots! They had learned nothing through the centuries! How slick she was as she lost her nerve, as she clambered back to terra firma, sweat and tears trickling down the hot aluminum.

"Since when did Jenna Faroli lack courage?" Her own voice in her fevered ear as she glared at her window. "Get a grip." She held tight and again began to mount the rungs. "Jenna Faroli, Queen of Tartoli." The ladder seemed sturdy. Up another step, and another—"Jenna Faroli, the Dame of the Bandwidth." Near the top she leaned over and, mustering her reserves, hoisted the sticky window, raising it an inch, another, another, resting, sucking in air, another inch, until it was open enough for her to get herself through. Now she had only to dive in headfirst. If the ladder held. If she didn't slip in the wide space between house and ladder. If she didn't fall once she was teetering on the sill, her top half in, her bottom hanging out.

There was no time that July quite like the window escapade, no time when she felt as reckless. Once she was inside her office, she sank down into the carpet, shaking, and sobbing with relief. She might have died. She might have died, and all for Charlie Rider. It would not have been worth it, such a death. Was she actually as strong as her feat proved her to be, or was she like a parent who performs a supernatural stunt in order to save her child? Her arms and legs were limp. Still trembling, she got up, changed her clothes, found her keys, and drove to the Kewaskum Inn, for a session that was, despite her fatigue and upset, possibly more profound than all the other assignations. How grateful he was that she had survived! How much he loved her for her near-sacrifice! When they were finished, she curled up next to him, and slept the divine sleep of the saved.

After the ladder incident, her message writing hardly seemed dangerous. What were a few smoochy e-mails compared with daredevil Jenna, seventeen feet in the air, catapulting her greasy self through a window? She knew she was writing, in a way, well beyond her feelings, and that he was, too, but the hyperbole was part of the game, part of the joy. And yet her feelings were basically sincere. She could blame the eleventh-century troubadours for inventing courtly love in the first place, for starting a tradition of excess. "I love you," she wrote to Charlie. "I love you before the Big Bang, I love you into the wormhole, I love you after all nothingness, I love you into the darkest reaches of the cell's intelligence, I love you into the mystery of the double helix, I love you into the repetition of the hexagon." Her high-school English teacher every now and again raised her painted black eyebrows. *Fuck you, Mrs. Billingsly. Fuck you, Strunk and White.*

"Have you lost weight?" Suzie Raditz said to her one morning as they walked down the hall toward the studio. "You look like you've shed about a gazillion pounds."

"I'm doing the South Beach for those—gazillion pounds," Jenna said. "Biting the bullet before menopause. It's brutal, but I guess it's working."

"I didn't mean you needed to lose a lot of weight, or even that you had weight to lose, I didn't mean—"

"It's okay, Suzie. I'm on a diet, it's effective, everything's fine." Jenna was having an unpleasant déjà vu, a clear memory of having had this same discussion about Suzie's weight, before the affair with David Oberhaus had been revealed.

"I'm just always so impressed when people get thin without personal trauma or falling in love. Frankly, those are the only ways I've ever slimmed down, the only ways—"

"She's in love with life, Suzie," Pete Warner said, from behind. He smashed his large frame up against the wall as he sidestepped past them. "Even so," he said to Jenna, "you still have a big ass."

"She does not. Jenna, you don't, I mean it's—"

Jenna opened the door to Studio B. "He's the only one around here who consistently speaks the truth."

"Okay," Suzie said, following her to the table. "Speaking of truth, I don't think we should do another gardening show. It was about five minutes ago that we had Stephanie Anderson, and who's this woman you want on—Laura Rider? Someone from your town? Phil is always doing the gardening-and-canning-and-fishing beat, and I swear to Jesus we don't need any more of that crap. Stephanie Anderson was one thing, because she's famous and she'd had her book, and she's best friends with Calvin and Ralph, and all those important, stylish fashionistas. But this Laura Rider, she's not anybody. I signed up for the Prairie Wind Farm online newsletter, and it's well done, but nothing amazing. Who in California is going to care about some farm in Nowheresville, Wisconsin?"

Jenna straightened her papers and sat down on her red chair. She was relieved to be back on track with Suzie. "Laura Rider's farm," she said, "is the most beautiful place I've ever been. It's fifty miles from here—a terrific, undiscovered destination. I'm going to have her for fifteen minutes on August 30, for my own pleasure. We will have no trouble, I assure you, finding an interesting angle. It will not be the end of the world."

"I'm just saying—"

"Thank you, Suzie. I appreciate it. Your instincts are good, and I understand your point. But I want to advertise something wonderful in our part of the state. For fifteen minutes, I'm not going to care about California or Massachusetts or Florida. Fifteen minutes." Once more she said, "It's not going to be the end of the world."

# Chapter 12

WHAT STRUCK LAURA MOST WAS THE BANALITY OF THE EX-changes. And that they both—all—had time for such schlock, and that their best efforts had so little creative spirit. They were saying things to each other that had been said by lovers through the ages, and yet they seemed to think they were inventing the concepts. That Jenna Faroli could be tedious was a shock, to be sure, and a disappointment, but, then, maybe the lesson was that love itself was tedious and disappointing. Love reduced the wooer and the wooed to no one more interesting than a baby rolling around in fecal matter. Even Jenna's large words and long sentences did not really do that much to dress up or make fascinating *I love you*. There was only so much a person could do on that score, and they'd already exhausted the genre. Laura supposed that she should take some responsibility, for having blazed the trail, but she had merely been channeling Charlie, and since then she was simply following in the gruesome twosome's footsteps. She wondered if the core conflict in their romance was the fact that they were unbearably dull.

Into July, she found herself skimming the messages and writing back cursorily. She was sure they were sleeping together when the message came through in which Jenna referred to their parts with proper names. Laura felt hardly a jolt, no real bombshell, because, frankly, she wanted to puke. Harvey for his, Gloria for hers. Gloria! As if Jenna's privates were the lead song in the ecstatic and reverent tradition of the Roman Catholic Mass. She was embarrassed for Jenna, embarrassed for Charlie, embarrassed for anyone who had ever done the same thing; she was embarrassed for being alive. The two of them were so proud of their accomplishments, as if, together, Harvey and Gloria had painted *The Last Supper* or performed *The Nutcracker* or written *As I Lay Dying*. They'd humped for hours, which was not, she should inform them, performance art or service to the Pope. It was nothing except a way to catch an infection or expire from boredom, nothing but a route to death.

She wondered now and again how she would get her characters through the long hot summer day of their affair, how she would keep the reader's attention if she had to include the lovers' endless kissy-face claptrap. It would have been so much better, she thought, if Don Juan and his patootie had waited awhile before they had sexual congress, if the lead-up to rubbing the bacon had been longer. It made her mad that they'd short-changed her experiment, but she had to keep reminding herself that her romance wouldn't concern itself with that part of the relationship, that her novel would be all courtship and coming into self-knowledge, all foreplay. There would be the Black Moment, and then the story would end with the final self-illumination and the wedding. Her book would not deal with the irksome rest of life.

It was perhaps to spice up her own interest in the exchanges that she began to insert herself more forcefully into the messages. One night at the beginning of July, she'd written to Jenna:

*Subj: Every song*
*From: crider@kingmail.com*
*To: JFaroli@wis.staff.edu*

*Darling,*
*I am making a mix tape for you. That's what people do who are going steady. I am making a tape that includes my old favorites as well as new tunes that remind me of you. Each one is for you. Each one is about you. Each one is everything I feel for you. Every song is you.*

The message was just the kind of idiotic prattle they'd been writing to each other four hundred times a day, but she thought with satisfaction that Charlie, when he read it, would blow a fuse. He'd storm through the house and then back up to his nook to do the mix tape, something he would wish he'd thought of on his own. She sent the message, and then she lay down on her sofa to think and to wait. She wondered if Jenna had overblown, violent fantasies. For instance, Jenna might wish that Laura would die slowly of natural causes, or that Laura and Frank Voden would smash into each other at the one traffic light in downtown Hartley, that they'd perish in the same accident. After a decent interval, the lovers could get married. Or Jenna might envision a weeper wherein Laura would phone in the middle of the night to say that Charlie had fallen down the stairs, and Jenna was the only person he wished to see before he drew his last breath. Mrs. Voden would arrive at the bedside, and they'd have a very special, a very beautiful parting.

Laura thought that, in reality, when your spouse died it would probably be like having a gangrenous arm amputated, that even though the limb had been diseased you'd still miss it.

Five minutes later: "What the fuck!" Charlie cried from upstairs. "Laura, what the fuck!"

So Jenna had written back to him something about the mix tape, and he'd seen Laura's initial message on the subject pasted into the response. E-mail, Laura said to herself, was so gratifyingly thorough and quick.

"What the fuck are you doing?" he shouted as he came rushing down the stairs in his adorable cat-pajama bottoms and a Green Bay Packers T-shirt. That was her husband, calibrated exquisitely, male and female together.

"What's the matter?" She lay with her hand over her eyes, resting in the balm of Jenna's fantasy, in the idea of herself dead and gone in order that the couple might have their happiness.

Charlie had already made Jenna a mixed CD. He wasn't going to tell Laura that he had burned one two weeks before that included, yes, his old favorites, his new favorites, each one in some way, it's true, embodying his feelings for Jenna. Did he have to inform his wife every time he said hello to Jenna, every time he gave her a posy, every time he wrote down an original line? Had she sniffed out the fact that he'd done this thing in secret, or had she been spying on him? Was she psychic or psycho? Jenna had written him back about the tape just then, clearly scratching her head, saying, "Dearest, you already made me the most magnificent compilation. You know how much I love it. You haven't forgotten that, have you?"

Laura had a silken gold shawl over her, and an enormous book on her stomach. Jenna often talked about Laura's beauty, but in the moment it was not visible to him. There was a smugness in the corners of her mouth, a taunt in the slight upward curve of her lower lip.

He made a superhuman effort to speak calmly. "I thought," he said, "I heard the barn door slamming. In the wind." She still had that look on her face. "Did you leave it open?"

"Did I leave it open? I think"—she turned the page of her book—"that if anyone left the barn door open, Charlie, it was you."

He almost said, I have a secret but I'm not going to tell you. He could have elaborated, could have said, I happen to know that Jenna is going to do something for you. Something exceptional, something she doesn't do for very many people. Maybe now, unfortunately, she'll change her mind. Maybe now, for whatever reason, it won't happen. Ha, he wanted to say. Ha. Under the present conditions, however, what could he do but turn on his heel and pound up the stairs? What could he do but begin to work on another CD, every song another portrait of his very own Jenna?

What I need to do, Laura thought after he'd gone, is sign up for the writing workshop in the Dells over Labor Day. There were workshops in all the genres: romance, mystery, self-help, literary, memoir, western, children's, poetry, creative nonfiction, and, the brochure said, so much more. Charlie had been having his fun, and she would have no problem informing him that she was leaving for four days to follow her bliss.

⌒

"Your wife is so lovely," Jenna said once more, a few days later, in bed, beneath the picture of a mesa and a lone chief with his horse in the glow of a very pink and very orange setting sun. She thought it the worst kind of art, solemnity in bright colors, but there was something right, under the circumstances, about the sincerity of the trashiness.

Charlie said nothing.

"Does she know how lovely she is?" Jenna was sitting atop him, leaning over and holding his head in her hands. He had unfastened all nine of her barrettes, and her long dark hair hung down her back and around her face. She had deeply etched crows' feet, and parenthetical lines at the corners of her mouth. She looked to him, with her mass of hair, like a creature—a good creature—out of mythology, a goddess who had laughed a great deal in her life. He wanted to tell her that he loved the way time and her nature had marked up her face.

"Most women don't believe they're gorgeous," he said, tracing her lips with his index finger. "Most women have no idea. It's ridiculous, how much they don't know. It's dumb of them, and sad."

"I want . . ." she began. Tears had sprung to her eyes. "I want to be beautiful to please you." It was horrifying to admit this, terrible, and yet it was the truest thing about her lying, cheating, sexing self. She had lost twenty pounds with no effort. Her eyes were larger now that they weren't hidden by the puff of her formerly fat cheeks. It seemed to her as if she'd taken one look at him, and in a breath shed several layers of Jenna Faroli. She had no appetite for food or sleep. She no longer read serious tomes about the war, the Middle East, the Administration, the climate. She was having trouble reading anything. Her mind was washed clean. She was thin, exhausted, and exhilaratingly vacant.

A week or so after Mrs. Rider's first mischief, after the CD episode, Laura wrote another meddling message.

*Subj: The Knees*
*From: crider@kingmail.com*
*To: JFaroli@wis.staff.edu*

*Lovey,*

*Did you know that in my knee there lives a family? Little Yardley Knee, the boy, and Samantha Knee, who is older than Yardley by two years, and Mrs. and Mr. Knee, and the valet, Gregory, who is a distant cousin, and his sister Mary Ruth Knee, the maid. There is an orphan nephew named Gerald Knee. Today Mr. and Mrs. Knee are celebrating their 17th wedding anniversary by not speaking to each other. I don't know why I haven't mentioned this before. There is probably, matter of fact, a family in your knee, too, that might want to come and visit my knee. I love you, C*

Laura had read a novel in which a gay couple invented a family who lived in their elbows. Because they were never going to adopt, never going to have the trouble of children to invigorate their dinner conversations, they were always inventing drama for the make-believe family, the Elbows, who had taken up residence in their joints. Laura could understand this need for daily spice. She and Charlie had their cat kingdom, starring their real-life cats, Polly, Mighty, Shawna, and Doofer. Polly had gone to the prom with the enormous feral tiger down the road, a bad boy named Julius. She had come in late with a bite on her ear—such a whore! It seemed to Laura that if Jenna and Charlie had characters they could share, their messages might become more interesting. This prodding them to enjoyment seemed to her yet another act of her own generosity. She was sure Jenna would take to it, that Jenna would be grateful.

And what do you know? Ten minutes later:

*Subj: Re: The Knees*
*From: JFaroli@wis.staff.edu*
*To: crider@kingmail.com*

*Oh God, dearest, you are so funny, so brilliant, so you. So you. SO YOU. Are the Knees not speaking because Mary Ruth Knee, as usual, has pitted Mother and Father against one another, because, wicked girl that she is, it was she who broke the Ming Dynasty vase (why are vases always from the Ming Dynasty?) and yet blamed it on Gerald, and the parents have taken sides? Or am I wrong? I love how you reveal your facets bit by bit. You draw, you sing, there is of course Harvey!—and, as always, your pure whimsy is on the tip of your sensational tongue. I love you, I love you.*

Laura had known Jenna would take to it like a duck to water, a pig to shit, a horse being led to the trough *and* drinking. Charlie was fully capable of inventing this kind of garbage himself, and she was merely speeding up the process, reminding him of his own talents, his *facets*.

At dinner, the Riders ate without speaking. He had grilled hamburgers, and they had baby carrots and potato chips, the sound of which, when being chewed, and no one was talking, filled the echo chamber of their heads. At the end of the meal, after he had drained his beer, and carefully set his glass down on its coaster, he looked at her midriff, raising his eyes a notch to her sternum, another to her clavicle, up the neck, until, finally, he rested his gaze on the shining face of his beloved wife. She was wearing the diamond earrings he'd given her for Christmas. "The Knees," he said.

She nodded. "The Knees."

They rose from the table, put the dishes in the sink, and went to their computers, one upstairs, the other down, to commence the evening correspondence.

# Chapter 13

CHARLIE AND JENNA HAD NEVER EATEN A REAL MEAL TO-
gether, and so, at the beginning of August, when Frank
went to Washington, the two arranged to have dinner in the
city. They would never, probably, be granted a whole night
through, and the evening in a restaurant would have to serve
as a token of the dream life. The plan had seemed a good one
a few days earlier, but in the hours before it, Jenna was not
sure. She had considered inviting him to the house and had
decided she wasn't up to the smell of him in the rooms, his
fragrance something she'd have to flap out afterward, opening
the windows, swishing away the smoke of him. She did not
want her sin in Frank's kitchen.

She was sitting at the table in the trattoria when Charlie
came along on the other side of the street. His washed and
pressed self was gleaming from half a block away, his Bora

Bora cologne no doubt wafting down the avenue. She felt her heart tighten. He was wearing a creamy linen sports coat with light-gray trousers, and—she squinted—sandals with socks? As if he suddenly had become Italian to match the restaurant. Surely, she thought just then, surely all of him was the work of Mrs. Rider. Who were these people, the Riders! His hair would have product squirted lightly through it to make his curls more vivid. Softer but also bold. Like Charlie himself. Soft but bold. Two qualities that were not complementary.

When he came through the door, she stood and, leaning over the table, the two kissed quickly. "You look so beautiful, so beautiful." He spoke in one low gusty breath, shaking his head in wonderment. That he was nervous made her heart go colder. It was unlikely that she was beautiful, especially in her present mood. She watched him taking up his napkin, unfolding it and spreading it carefully on his lap. "I like this place," he whispered conspiratorially. "Leave it to you to find a restaurant like this, to discover it, to realize a good thing when you see it. They know you here, I'll bet—I'll bet they know exactly what you—"

The waiter had arrived at the table. "Good evening, gentlemens," he said to Charlie. "I like very much, ah, to see you tonight."

"Same here!" Charlie said. "It's great to see you, too."

Jenna had never hated him before. It had been wrong, she realized, to expose him to the light, to remove him—to remove them—from the Kewaskum Inn, that sanctuary for their most private selves. *"Carlo, per favore, per incominciare, voglio forse caponata, prosciutto, e olivi, va bene? E una bottiglia di vino bianco, forse un Pino Grigio o un buon Orvieto, d'accordo?"*

Carlo bowed and retreated. Charlie was staring at her. "Your voice in Italian. It's even, it's even more incredible than your English voice. You are—"

"My Italian allowed me to order wine and appetizers. This is not unimportant, but it has its limitations." They should have met at a bar near Hartley. It would have been easy to feign innocence, and on his turf she could have happily gobbled up chicken wings and had beer by the pitcher. Although she had already made her choices, she studied the menu. "You once used *pasta e fagioli* in a rhyme to me," she muttered.

Without thinking, he said, "The contribution of Mrs. Rider."

"What?"

Jenna, he would admit, did not look as lovable when her brow was wrinkled, her frown lines were so severe, and she let her mouth hang open. "She had that dish at a restaurant when she was sixteen and has never stopped talking about it— Golly, you look good." He was leaning halfway across the table. "I love your dress, the brownness of it, and the buttons. It looks French, not that I know what a French dress looks like, but if a dress could look French, then this dress does. The buttons remind me of Milk Duds. Do you remember eating Milk Duds and how they'd get mashed together into one gluey lump on the roof of your mouth? I love those buttons, I could eat them, I love the idea of you—"

"Stop!" she cried. "Please." She had startled him away from the center of the table, startled him into the corner of his chair. "It's probably best," she went on, "if I order for both of us. That is, if you don't mind."

"I'll love whatever you decide," he said slowly, adjusting himself, coming forward, advancing a little. "Darling," he added. He picked up the small bottle of olive oil next to the vase of begonias and he smiled at it, which made her dislike him even more. "How are you?" he murmured, as he replaced the bottle.

She laughed then, at the absurdity of him, the absurdity of the dinner, and it had not even yet begun. She laughed at how she'd fallen into all the love traps—imagining that the affair could go on forever, that their feelings would always be fresh, imagining that somehow they would grow old together in their separate households. Poor dumb Jenna and poor Charlie, the yokel. Poor unsuspecting Laura and Frank; poor Suzie and David Oberhaus; poor Vanessa, far from home.

"How am I?" she said. "Yesterday a colleague of mine tried to kill himself. I'd had warning about this from my producer, but I'd dismissed her without hearing her out." David Oberhaus had taken an overdose of pain pills, just, apparently, as Suzie had feared. He had done this at home after his wife had phoned the program director at the station, telling him about Suzie. David's daughter, another poor girl, had found him in time, so that he could wake up in the hospital to more shame. "I don't know that I could have prevented it," Jenna said, "but I should have listened to Suzie's appeal. Probably I should have listened. I don't know. I don't know anything anymore."

She stared at the centerpiece as she spoke. "And Vanessa. She falls in love at the drop of a hat. The boyfriends either have no ambition or no sense of humor or no job, or else they work all the time. She needs to ditch her Ph.D. and go to choosing school." If only there were choosing school! It was remarkable how some of Vanessa's friends went about their sex lives as if intercourse were on a to-do list, and when it didn't suit, they easily cast aside the beau and found another, or did volunteer work instead. They seemed not to be vulnerable to beauty. "Also," Jenna went on, "she sprained her wrist, so she's having trouble doing simple tasks in the lab. Her purse was stolen in the emergency room, and she's worried about identity theft. She can't seem to get up in the morning without having a crisis. I can't leave at the moment, can't rush to St. Louis to hold her wounded hand."

"You're a good mother," he said. "That's obvious."

"Obvious?" She snapped the menu shut. "I did the best I could, but that's saying very little." She should not have told him about David Oberhaus or about Vanessa. She never talked about Frank; Frank had nothing whatsoever to do with Charlie Rider. And Vanessa: even if Jenna wanted to, how could she explain the tailspin Vanessa could send her mother into by being disappointed in the seasoning of her entrée or sneezing or having a lonely day? Furthermore, Jenna could never admit that every now and then, for the smallest, sharpest measure of time, she wished for a different child, a better child, a child who was not as difficult.

Carlo soon brought the wine and the eggplant and olives. Jenna ordered for both of them: the pappardelle, and veal chops with garlic and anchovies, and boiled zucchini salad, which, she explained to Charlie, tasted far better than it sounded.

"Cool," Charlie said.

The wine was nicely fruity with a mineral follow-through and a clean finish. She began to feel better despite Charlie's having said *Cool.* "Love is merely a madness," she thought, "and . . . something, something . . . deserves as well a dark house and a whip as madmen do." If Frank were along, he'd quote many of Rosalind's lines, his favorite heroine in all of Shakespeare. If Frank were here—how ashamed she'd be. She took another swallow and for a moment closed her eyes. "Does your wife dress you, dear Charlie Rider?" She had always meant to ask.

"I am outfitted daily by Herself. Sometimes I am draped two or three times an hour by Mrs. Rider. I am her Ken doll."

Jenna laughed. "Why do you let her?"

"Why do I let her?"

"Are you afraid of her?"

He took four bites, each a toothful, to polish off a small niçoise olive. "In a way, I probably am," he said.

"What way?" Jenna said. She was beginning to enjoy herself.

"I'm afraid of a force in her. A force that is always there but lying low. A force that could spring up at any moment."

"What kind of force?"

"Dissatisfaction, maybe, I'd call it. Unhappiness coiled and at the ready? Or rage, waiting in the wings?"

She wouldn't say, but that was exactly the problem with Vanessa.

"I'll tell you one thing. I'd like to tell you one thing, and that is, if I could go backward in time, I'd have children. I would have liked to be a father." He was gazing into the street as if there before him were lined up the tykes of an alternative life.

"Charlie!" she said, touching his hand. He would have been as boyish and playful as his sons, all of them running around the yard after fireflies on a summer night, all of them tumbling into a hammock. She covered her mouth, and then, of all the terrible thoughts she'd had so far that hour, she entertained the worst: she imagined having Charlie's baby, she, without a womb and nearly over-the-hill, bearing him a miracle, a rotund version of himself, a baby with luscious thighs and fat little fists, and the tear-shaped eyes, and a happy, toothless smile. She put her head into her napkin and—how mad!—began to cry.

"Honey, sweetie, it's all right, it's okay." He reached over to stroke her forearm.

"But why didn't you?" she choked. "Why didn't you have them?"

"We made the decision not to spend the money and the time on Laura's issues. Scar tissue down there, and a screwy cycle. We decided to concentrate on the farm and to enjoy our nieces and nephews. Laura has never liked doctors, and to her it didn't seem worth it, the pain, the money, when there are enough people on the globe."

Jenna wiped her eyes. The abstraction of doing good by not having children surely was cold comfort. As miserable as Vanessa often was, Jenna couldn't bear the thought of the world without her child in it.

As she was considering what subject to put forth next, he reached into his pocket and retrieved several folded sheets of paper. "I made these for you," he said, handing her the packet.

He had drawn portraits of the Knee family, Yardley in his shorts, Mary Ruth in a pinafore, Gerald looking downtrodden, as an orphan must, the parents beleaguered but loving. He had inked the drawings and filled them in with soft greens and blues and violets. "Charlie, oh, Charlie," she whispered. How was it that he had filled her heart with hate one minute and won her back in the next?

The pappardelle came in its sauce of red and yellow peppers and sausages, and she moved the portraits out of the way. They were like drawings in an Edwardian children's book, the outlines crisp, the girls in dresses, their hair in pigtails. He'd folded them up, as if he hadn't thought enough of them to keep them uncreased, but they were beguiling, full of charming details, Yardley with a snake hanging out of his pocket, the mother holding her purse in front of her with both hands, the dog itching a flea, the butler's cravat askew. Jenna said, "I can't figure out how I got here."

Charlie understood her meaning. "My wife," he said. "My wife always wanted us to be friends."

Jenna put her fork down. "She did?"

"She had a feeling we'd like each other."

"But we met by accident. We ran into each other on Highway S."

"That," he said, "was the Silver People."

"But how—?" She opened up the drawings again. Looking at them was like taking a sip of the love potion. One glance at Yardley Knee, at the accomplishment of the drawing, and she was his. She released herself into the world of Charlie Rider. She would keep referring to the papers through the pappardelle, and the veal, and the coffee, and once more when they were back at the Faroli-Voden house, in the guest room, where, she'd decided, she must bring him after all.

"Does Laura know about the Knees?" she whispered as he unbuttoned her shirt.

Charlie kissed Jenna's neck. He wanted to be honest, and so he said what seemed truthful—in spirit, anyway. "Laura is in my knee right now," he muttered. "Laura is always in my fucking knee."

# Chapter 14

THE NIGHT BEFORE LAURA WAS GOING TO BE ON THE *JENNA Faroli Show*, she was working on the Prairie Wind Farm newsletter. It was a bad habit, she knew, to have as many windows open on her desktop as she did, and for sure a person could get confused. It was late, and although she was tired she was too excited to sleep, and also the newsletter was overdue. Best to get it done while she had adrenaline.

She'd been following Jenna's correspondence more carefully in the last week, since, after all, she was going to be on the program. Not that there seemed to be anything particularly new, except that Jenna and Charlie must have had some kind of intense, intergalactic sexual experience. Mrs. Voden was more ardent than usual. If there was anything to be interested in, it was how free Jenna felt when she wrote, as if she believed she was always unobserved. Laura understood very little about her own software, but she was savvy enough to suspect that everyone could be observed: the server could spy on you, and so could the twelve-year-old neighbor boys, the local government, the federal government, and the terrorists. Jenna could get excruciatingly specific without, it seemed, the thought of a peeping Tom. That evening, in fact, she'd written a doozy.

It wasn't so much the physical details that got to Laura, although she found them gross in the extreme. The way Jenna wrote about her pleasure, you would have thought that no one had ever touched her down there, that she'd lived her life in a convent. You would have thought that she'd only just realized, at age forty-six, why people had been making art about sex, and going to war on account of it, and jeopardizing their careers for it. Jenna and her lightbulb moment. That delayed revelation would have been enough embarrassment, without all the other mortifications.

The message that Laura had open on her screen while she was writing her newsletter mentioned the effect on Jenna of Charlie's fluttering tongue, his focused tongue, all the *facets* of Charlie's tongue. Jenna had gone on to confide in him, to tell him that she'd been having the fantasy of carrying his child. "Jeez!" Laura spat when she read that line. Jenna wrote that through the nights she'd been dreaming of a small boy on the lawn, running and shrieking with delight as his father, Charlie, chased him. In the mornings, as Jenna woke, the feeling of the dream was still with her, the joy of it, and she'd lie in bed, she reported, imagining that this baby would bring all of them together, that she and Frank and Laura and Charlie would stand in a loving circle in the nursery. "That's sweet, I guess," Mrs. Rider remarked to her laptop. "I know," Jenna had written, "that the castle-building is goofy if not perhaps pathological."

"Pathologically goofy," Laura clarified.

If Jenna had been younger, Mrs. Rider might well have felt threatened, but as it was she registered the message as the work of someone who had gone far beyond reason. If the part about the baby and the other bit about oral sex hadn't been enough for one message, Jenna also spoke about growing old together, being on the same wing of the nursing home:

> I imagine you are down the hall, and the nurse will wheel me, poor old Jenna Faroli, to Charlie Rider's room in the evening, and although I remember almost nothing it is you who I know, you who I recall, you who I love. I hope that in spite of the scarcity of men in nursing homes, in spite of the fact that all the old bags are throwing themselves at you, you still hold me in your heart. I like to think the nurses will be compassionate enough to lift me into your bed, that they will leave us, that they will shut the door behind them.

Laura hooted. Finally, the couple united! She clapped. Finally, the couple gets to spend the night together! More applause. She loved this last section—she adored this derangement—the marriage of the demented and the crippled. Some romance all right, the false teeth smiling at false teeth in two glasses, side by side, on the table. And what about Laura? Where was she going to be while the seniors diddled themselves? Was she having her heavenly reward? Or was she the remaining friend and relation, the long-suffering visitor, bringing mints and reading stories and making sure their drool buckets hadn't gotten dislodged?

It was peculiar, she knew, that by day, when Laura was listening to the radio, Jenna Faroli was entirely separate from Charlie's Jenna, from Mrs. Voden. Jenna Faroli was her usual enlightened and wise self beaming down upon them, educating the world. The other Jenna, the lunatic lover, was, in Laura's mind, someone else. Laura supposed that she had learned a few things that would be useful to her for her book, but it seemed that Jenna actually hadn't been that instructive; a romance, after all, was supposed to be empowering rather than confusing and nauseating.

She would later say it was an honest mistake. There were too many windows open on her desktop. And she was rattled because she was going to be on the show the next day. She had meant to paste into her newsletter a small piece she'd written about making autumn arrangements, including a photograph of a pot et fleur she'd done the year before with oak, maple, and a few deciduous azalea leaves. She absolutely did not mean to paste Jenna's message into the front page, and even though she always proofread, the hour was late. She did not mean, without rereading, to send the newsletter to the 637 customers on the LISTSERV.

# Chapter 15

WHEN JENNA CAME INTO STUDIO B THE FOLLOWING MORN-
ing, Laura noticed that she was flushed, and her eyes, which
she remembered as a calm gray, looked like hot little ball
bearings. Jenna said, "How are you?" without glancing across
the table, so that, even though Laura was the only one in
the studio, she wasn't sure the question had been directed
at her. The producer Suzie, the woman who had done the
telephone pre-interview the day before, had said that Jenna
usually came in five or ten minutes before the show to talk
with the guest, but the wall clock said 9:58:07, hardly allowing time for pleasantries.

Laura, shoulders to her ears and grinning, clenched every
part of herself. "I—I'm excited to be here."

Jenna's blazing eyes were fixed on the producer in the control room. Laura could see Suzie, head down, at her laptop.

"We'll just chat," Jenna said, as if to the window, "see where it takes us."

Laura nodded. On the phone, Suzie had said they would talk a little bit about unusual flower names and the spiritual aspects of working with plants that had a long heritage, and the benefits of being surrounded by beauty. They had brainstormed, and it had gone, Laura thought, pretty well. She had come armed with a list of her favorite plants as well as those with odd names. She had studied up, but if Jenna Faroli wanted to just chat, Laura, thrilled to the bone, scared out of her mind, could do that, too.

Jenna whacked her papers on the table and sat in the spot next to Laura, so that both of them would have to swivel a bit in their chairs to conduct the conversation. She put her headset on, and to the engineer she said through her mike, "I'm all right on the levels?" She studied her notes, licked her finger to turn a page, and took a drink of water.

At 9:59:57, she turned her gaze on Laura. It was slightly unnerving—the eyes, for one, and the hard, wide, close-mouthed smile. She was smaller than Laura remembered, and possibly prettier? She'd managed to corral her hair into an upswept structure, a bunnish thing somewhere between a French twist and the Great Pyramids, and she was wearing a beige brushed-cotton suit, and heels, so that her clothing, at least, was not so far from the vision Laura used to have of her, before they'd met. It made total sense that Jenna's cheeks would burn under the pressure of the show, and of course she would be businesslike rather than friendly before the program went on air.

"Here we go, then," Jenna said. She looked, Laura realized, as if she were going to vomit, and in a certain way this made Laura feel good, to know that Jenna was nervous, too. She was glad not to be across the table but next to her host, as if they were seatmates traveling to the same destination.

The jaunty Jenna Faroli music, the signature loopy, playful clarinet, sounded in Laura's headset. She squeezed her eyes shut. She hadn't known what to wear, how dressy it should be, and she'd chosen a flowered knee-length skirt, a pouffy thing, roses splashed on the pale-yellow seersucker, and a silk tank top of the same yellow. It was garden-theme–y, festive, and yet serious, which was how she wanted to feel. If it was an outfit a schoolgirl would wear, well, that was part of the picture. The producer had told her that she was first, and next there'd be an author who had written a book about growing vegetables with prison inmates, and following that a phone interview with a director who staged Shakespeare plays with convicted felons, and, last, Jenna would discuss the Bard with another author, a man who'd written a biography of the playwright, and an exegesis, Suzie had called it, of the plays in relation to the flora of the times. Always, in a Jenna show, there was a flow and a circle. Just now Suzie had been very interested in the Riders' business, and she'd asked quite a few questions about the current newsletter, which Laura had to confess she'd patched together late the evening before.

"You don't say," Suzie had said.

"I have with me in the studio Laura Rider," Jenna was saying, "co-owner of Prairie Wind Farm in Hartley, Wisconsin. It's one of the most enchanting places I've ever visited. Ms. Rider designs gardens, and has a showcase on the farm that will transport you to another era and another continent."

Jenna had gone from being fierce and commanding, gone from looking ill, to her warm and inviting self. Laura took a deep breath and smiled gratefully at her. She sent out yet another prayer that she would be able to speak in whole sentences, that she'd be able to do justice to this experience.

"Your farm is a masterpiece," Jenna said, "of design and execution. It is a place of great tranquillity and peace for visitors, and yet it must afford *you* little time for peace and quiet."

Laura nodded, and then realized that of course she needed to speak. "It—is a lot of work, absolutely, but we, my husband and I, we have some time for hobbies, we do. I'm actually— what I love, Jenna—is to write, I—really do. I'm planning, in fact, to write a book. I'm sort of, well, I'm already at work on a novel." Eeeek! She was telling her secret to Jenna! *Pinch me!* "So it seems sort of fitting that I'm on this show today, which is about writing—about Shakespeare, a glove maker's son, right?—as well as gardening." What a mouthful! But she'd said it; she'd told Jenna who she was.

Jenna's gaze, narrowed now, and focused as if to a pinprick, was, needless to say, intense, but when you factored in the voice like a flute, plus the smile, you could sort of

relax. Maybe, Laura thought, Jenna's eyes looked so pen-
etrating because it was there, in her pupils, that her thinking
was expressed. Some people talked in order to think, some
people could only understand their ideas if they wrote them
down, Charlie's irises flooded with love, and Jenna's eyes went
into laser mode when she did her interviews. Everything was
logical!

"Writing a book," Jenna said slowly, as if this were a concept that was unknown to her. "How fascinating."

"It is amazing."

"Have you always been a reader, then? Were you one of
those girls who were up a tree somewhere, nose in a book?"

"No, not at all. I was so average back then. My family
thought I was pretty hopeless. I liked animals, and arts and
crafts, and dolls, and then, you know"—she didn't mean to
giggle, but a little high hee-hee escaped her—"boys."

"Not a reader," Jenna purred, "and yet you want to
write."

"I used to read, you know, for facts, but I started in with
novels, with those kinds of books, reading them, a few years
ago, and I got very very hooked."

Jenna cocked her head and adjusted her mike so she could
lean toward Laura. It was just how Laura used to imagine
Jenna when she listened; it was actually true that you could
hear Jenna's curiosity. "So you feel as if you can write a novel
even though you haven't trained for it all your life. I'm sure
you are aware that we live in a culture of the amateur, a

culture where everyone thinks he is an artist. You blog and you're a poet. Didn't George Bernard Shaw say that hell is filled with amateur musicians? Most writers I've interviewed on this show report that they've read since their earliest years, and either they studied literature in college or they read seriously for decades before taking pen to paper. Many of them have spoken about how in the act of writing they are having conversations with authors long dead and with the books themselves. They are part of a specific history and continuum. And yet you feel you can read up, for a year or two, and then sit down and write a book?"

Laura could tell by how close Jenna had come and her look of concern that she truly wanted to know what Laura thought. It was personal and intellectual, at the same time. "I do feel I can do it," she said. "Anyone can if they believe hard enough. If they follow their bliss. That's the greatest thing about writing. It's not rocket science. It's not some in-joke with other writers or books. It's storytelling, something we all do, all of us, every day. I do believe we are all writers. Every glove maker's son can be a poet."

"Surely not every glove maker's—"

"Stranger things have happened, trust me. And because, Jenna, I've been working on a romance novel, I've been watching classics like *Pride and Prejudice* with Keira Knightley, movies like that. Doing, you know, catch-up."

"Classics," Jenna repeated. "Keira Knightley." She seemed to be getting information from her producer, from her feed, because she looked at Suzie, who was now standing at the window, and sternly shook her head. "What, I wonder, do you like about *Pride and Prejudice*, the movie, that classic, as you call it? In this current Austen revival, it's assumed that we all understand she's great and why this is so, but what do you, who have just come to her, have to say about that greatness?"

"Oh my gosh, the movie is so empowering. And happy. You really get that the hero and the heroine have made each other better people. Which I think is the point, right, of love? You probably next want to ask me if I've read a lot of romances, and the truth is, I haven't."

Jenna laughed her wonderful water-going-over-the-falls laugh, all bubbly and rolling. Laura's heart swelled, and her own cheeks, she was sure, were glowing. It was with merriment that Jenna said, "That does seem like trying to play a concert without ever practicing, without having tried to blow through your instrument!" And then, more seriously, "Many of the most successful romance writers started out as devoted readers of the genre, didn't they?"

"That makes sense. But for me, Jenna? The fact is, I don't like the usual plot where the independent, strong woman meets the stud-muffin who seems stupid or evil or stuck up, and after three hundred pages where the characters don't know what is what, and after he rapes her and gets to play around, after she shows him his pure side, he carries her off into the sunset. That just doesn't feel right to me. But I'm not sure I like the plot, either, where the hero is so strong he can let the woman rule, because that makes the heroine seem sort of like a brat. I want to write a book about all women, Every Woman. I want to find out what women want, deep down, and I want to discover what the ideal man is for today's real woman."

"The ideal man. Today's real woman." Jenna shook her head again, a sharp back-and-forth at the window. "That's very ambitious. How do you find out such a thing? How do you research, if you will, what Every Woman wants, or who Every Woman is?"

"How I look at it is, a writer has to be a sleuth. It's detective work. I've been trying to study, to study what, in my opinion—in my humble opinion?—an ideal woman, a brilliant and amazing woman, actually wants in a man, what kind of hero she needs when she's already sort of perfect. Because, Jenna, today's women are superevolved. I don't need to tell you that! They run their own businesses, they raise children alone, they take charge of their own learning. If women need men, why do they? What kind of man can improve the new model? What kind of partner can take her to new heights? That's what my research is about. And if the artist has to snoop a little bit and create opportunities, if you have to listen very hard to the people around you and watch, that's all part of the process."

Laura would remember how the room went still, how it was as if Jenna had been in a game of tag, as if she'd been made to freeze by an invisible hand. What had just happened? Laura could hardly remember, sentence to sentence, what was coming out of her mouth. She'd never experienced living in the moment as she was doing now. She almost said to Jenna, "Are you okay?" but she thought it might be better if she continued to talk. "I listened to the show you did about a year ago—I mean, I listen to you every day!—but a while back you interviewed an author who'd written a book about romance readers. I probably won't get this straight, but the author—if I'm remembering correctly—said that romance readers and the heroines in the books, too, seem to be searching for a hero with the kind of tenderness and love they got from their mothers. I just thought that was so interesting, that longing for mother-love and trying to find it in a man. I mean, good luck! The author made the point that in most romances the hero is masculine in terms of his . . . equipment, but actually feminine in—what would you call it?—his emotional capacity. His feminine and masculine sides are . . . calibrated exquisitely. I guess I've been thinking of that a lot, maybe without even knowing I've been thinking of it, which is how an artist goes about her life and work. The thing is, I want to write a romance where the characters are fully conscious as they enter the relationship. Really, truly, fully conscious."

For a second, Laura felt dizzy. She had never spoken like that, in a full paragraph, one that she hoped was coherent. Jenna still hadn't moved. Was she having a stroke? Was she like that actor, what's-his-name, who for all those years performed in his sitcom while in secret he had Parkinson's disease? Laura felt bad about bringing up the idea that women were searching for their mothers when Jenna, after all, had been adopted. She wished she could scoot her chair over to the motherless child and take her in her arms.

"A conscious romance." Jenna was finally speaking, drawing out the *s* sounds, hissing the words.

"Yes! Oh my goodness, that's it! The conscious romance! That's exactly the name of the new genre I'm planning to invent. Thank you!!!"

Jenna blinked, sat up straight, and seemed, Laura later thought, to go into an autopilot-type mode. "Studies have been done"—she was still blinking—"which show that romance novels, while often ideologically conservative, while often recommending the patriarchy, are, for many women, an activity of protest." Her eyes popped open and she said, "Have you researched that aspect of the genre in order to understand what propaganda, if you will, your book will espouse?"

"I feel like I'm living in my book," Laura said, "that my book is from deep inside me, that it's an expression of myself rather than a—what did you call it?—rather than propaganda? I've listened to your show for years, and I know that artists make great sacrifices, and I myself, believe me, have sacrificed, more than anyone can imagine, more than anyone will ever know. But I feel that it's meant to be. I've had this fantasy for years that I'm sitting in a chair, in a long dress, with a cup of tea by my side, and a cigarette in an ashtray. And I'm writing."

Jenna thrust her head forward and squinted at her. "Just as Nicole Kidman does in the movie *The Hours*, when she's playing Virginia Woolf? When she's writing *Mrs. Dalloway*?"

"Uh-huh," Laura said vaguely.

It was as if, just then, Jenna woke back up into herself. Maybe she had some kind of seizure disorder and the crisis had passed. She pulled her mike closer to her, turning away from Laura, and she said to the window, "You've got all the visual trappings of Virginia Woolf without, of course, knowing Greek, or being well-read, or having a literary circle. But you would no doubt say that everyone needs her fantasies, and the movies are a good place to get them."

"Absolute—"

"And you believe that what women want has fundamentally changed through the eons, through the feminist revolution, and now into the third wave of that revolution, when poststructuralist interpretation of gender and sexuality is central to the discussion. I'm sure you've looked at queer theory, womanism, postcolonial theory, ecofeminism, the riot-grrrl movement, to name but a few."

"You make it sound so intense! I'm just trying to tell a story about love, about what kind of love we all need in the twenty-first century."

"What kind of love we need, no matter if we're oppressed in third-world countries, if we live in a war-torn place, if we have no access to birth control, if we're illegal immigrants or transgendered. What kind of love we need—" Suzie had tiptoed into the studio to hand a piece of paper to Jenna, at which, Laura noted, Jenna did not so much as glance. "You seem to be saying that women's nature has changed dramatically. The new female model, as you call it, is a far cry from, say, Shakespeare's heroines. In your book there will be no lover's hysterics, no tension borne from misunderstanding, no subduing of one of the partners. No more shrews, no more domineering women, no hectoring missus who drives the mister to the grave. Love itself will be transformed. Love itself will no longer be a madness."

"There's got to be a better way, Jenna, to live together."

"And yet your methods for writing this book prove that you yourself, the artist, are still fixed in one of the old models of woman, if you will. Laura Rider, the conniver." Jenna smiled so lovingly. "Laura Rider, the snoop, as you called yourself. The manipulative vixen. A ruthless b—"

"I'm just trying—"

"Let me get this straight." Jenna's voice had gone down a notch in pitch, and had become even smoother. "You never read a novel before the age of forty-three. You think you're getting educated by watching Jane Austen movies. You don't have any sense of American letters. You don't have an idea of the tradition even in your chosen genre. You seem to have the idea that Every Woman is a white middle-class female searching for love, and, further, you believe that your experience is deep enough for you to write a story that has universal appeal."

"I hope—"

"I'm afraid we're out of time. Good luck to you, Laura Rider. Perhaps you are the model of today, not just of the female but of the American. The person of the moment, this moment, when a cowboy can be president and you need no talent to be a celebrity. You need only be a narcissist in order to brutalize your husband. Or your neighbor. Laura Rider, *folks*, is so attractive she'll no doubt be featured in *People* and *Glamour* and *Vogue*." Jenna was talking over the music that had come on and ignoring the fact that Suzie was ushering in the next guest. "Her book is sure to be a blockbuster. Every Woman and the Ideal Hero. It will be a book, a TV series, a computer game, and there'll be action figures in our Happy Meals. She's sure to be a sensation, at least for a weekend. She's sure to be a Brand. Thank you, Laura Rider, for being with us."

"It—it was fantastic!" What Laura would give to squeeze Jenna's hand. "Thank you! Thank you so much."

# Chapter 16

IT WAS SOMETHING OF A COINCIDENCE THAT JENNA'S VACA-
tion with Frank began the day after the Laura Rider show.
If she'd been in a different frame of mind, that is, she might
have seen it as fortuitous: time off with her husband just when
she most needed it. She found herself, on Friday afternoon,
on the Outer Banks of North Carolina, in Sally and Dickie's
beach house, the four friends with a week ahead of leisure, the
four of them drinking and cooking and playing Scrabble in
living languages, the four of them talking up and down the
beach, talking the minute their feet hit the floor in the morning, talking the day long, talking up the stairs, talking as they
fell into their beds, into a deep sleep, their mouths still open.
Under the circumstances, however, she would have liked to
drive alone to a stark and lonely place, to the Badlands, to the

shores of a glacial lake in Alaska, no creatures there but the grizzly and the vulture.

She had meant to glance at her e-mail before the Thursday-morning show, to see if there was any word from Vanessa, and she'd noticed the Prairie Wind Farm newsletter from LPRider@prairiewind.com. She was standing at her desk in the office, leaning over the back of her chair, scrolling—

> . . . the tip of your tongue, a feather in the wind . . . Never has anyone . . . I have been dreaming about your child, our child, and how . . . I imagine you are down the hall, and the nurse will wheel me, poor old Jenna Faroli, to Charlie Rider's room in the evening. . . .

For an instant she couldn't see, the screen, a murky blue, the words fizzing up, the flash of *your child, our child, your tongue.* She held tight to the back of her chair. Her eyes—they were dry and hot, her lids sticky, the words coming in longer bursts. *Oh, but such a feather, your tongue, at once delicate, at once so strong.* She tried to look with greater discernment, eyes wide, because if she were seeing more clearly the message would not be there. She tried to blink. The communication, obdurate and whole, remained. What was it doing in the Prairie Wind newsletter? In the center of the first page? How had it gotten there? She was able to frame those questions. She was able next to think, Hahahahahaha. It was a joke, a Charlie hijink, a Silver Person prank. She scrolled to the top, and there was the official logo, the long grasses waving as if in the breeze, and the address of the sender. It was from Laura Rider. It was the newsletter. But it wouldn't have gone to anyone else, would it? Even though Jenna's heart was banging in her ears and her eyeballs themselves were stuck and pulsing—of course this was something only Jenna was privy to, a very private joke. But what if it wasn't? What if Laura Rider had found out? That was it, yes, Laura knew. Charlie had left his files open on his desktop, his wife had seen the message, she was in a fury, and she wanted Jenna to know she knew. Fair enough, this was retribution, a singular note to Jenna, everyone on the same page now. Laura would either be in the studio shortly and beating about Jenna's face and shrieking, or else she wouldn't show up. Think it through. Breathe deep. As the matter stood, therefore, wasn't it unlikely that a polite, reserved person such as Laura Rider would come for the interview?

She sat down and tried, again, to see, to read. *In my dream life our child brings all of us together. The places you touch me bring revelation and God.* Each sentence was more unspeakable than the last. *In the nursing home you come to feed me tapioca and you bring your kisses, too, soft as velvet, probing as* . . . She couldn't read on. She knew she was the author, but she could not now believe it. Had there been acid laced into her peach cobbler? What had she been thinking last night? What had she been thinking all these months? Who was she? Even as she questioned herself, even as she felt the smear over her heart, the hot tar of shame, she also recalled how she'd loved Charlie. She'd been overcome by sentiment, overcome by the long thick viper of tenderness, as she wrote about how she hoped a nurse would help her into Charlie's bed in the nursing home, as she imagined Charlie lifting their child up into the air in the sweet, cool spring evening.

The shadow across her screen was Suzie Raditz in the door, Suzie standing, arms folded on her chest, her weight on one leg, the other crossed at the ankle. She was leaning against the jamb. She was staring at Jenna.

"Uhhh," Jenna said, clamping her eyes shut. Suzie, the star producer, thorough and up-to-the-minute, surely was on the newsletter listserv.

"We're fifteen minutes away. Your guest is here. Looking like a flower, like a fucking bouquet, actually. Prairie . . . Wind . . . Farm." She nodded slowly. "Your idea."

*Try to find the thrill in sound judgment.*

"Dear God," Jenna whispered.

"She's quite a writer."

"Close the door," Jenna managed, "will you please." She wished to be vaporized, to be expelled through a trapdoor into some place that was not the state of Wisconsin, and furthermore, some place where her own basic self was gone. She had never before harbored the desire not to be, never felt the perfection of nonexistence. How hot were her cheeks, how red? She covered her moist face with her shaking hands. How ready the body was to broadcast its shame, the body always on high alert for the owner's idiocy. How many people, besides

Suzie, had read the newsletter? Had Frank? Not Vanessa, no, not her daughter! How many people could be on the mailing list of a small operation like Prairie Wind Farm? And not only that, oh no, not only that: how many newsletter readers would forward the message to their friends and relations? She put her head down on the desk to try, somehow, to get a grip. Was it the work of Charlie? Of course not! It was Laura who had written the newsletter. But why now, at this instant, right before the show?

A few minutes later, Suzie knocked and, without waiting for an answer, opened the door. "Do you need . . . help?" There was very little sarcasm in her voice.

"I'm fine," Jenna said into her hands. "Thank you. I'll be right there."

At home, after the show, she had planned to tell Frank, tell him the entire sordid tale, how she had been duped by Laura, by Charlie, and most of all by herself. She would explain the wretched unfolding, piece by piece. She would tell it without tears, without self-pity, without justifications. She would stick to the unadorned, repugnant facts.

Unfortunately, that night he'd been delayed at the office, and once he'd charged in—kissing her on the cheek, patting her hair—he'd gone straight upstairs to pack. She'd walked out into the yard to rehearse her speech again, and when she'd finally mounted the steps, one foot, the other, so heavy, her feet in the brown lace-up shoes, he was snoring in the middle of the made bed, in the middle of his stack of Tommy Bahama shirts and his boxer shorts.

It hadn't seemed right to tell him in the airport, or on the plane. In the rental car, on the way to the beach, she should have come clean. But the pressure of the story in her chest, in her frontal lobe, and right behind her eyes—the fact that the only thing beating in her was the story—made it impossible to think about telling it in any rational way. She was afraid she'd open her mouth to start talking and she'd bleat.

On the morning of the show, after Laura's segment, she'd somehow gotten through the rest of the program with the other guests. The interviews were a thick haze in her memory. It seemed to her that there was one caller who had asked why Jenna had been so hard on the young romance writer. It was as if she'd gone into a wood that was on fire and come out, nothing to look back to but the charred remains. She did recall reading the newsletter beforehand, and she remembered with terrible clarity watching Suzie in the control room during the newsbreak. Suzie had been showing something—and surely it was the newsletter—to Pete and Carol on her laptop. Suzie was doing this, Jenna knew, for Jenna's benefit, humiliating her in front of her staff. She could see Pete lean down to look, could see Pete frowning, saying, "What?" to Suzie, and looking again. Suzie, eyebrows raised, nodded and kept nodding her confirmation. *Didn't I always say she was a bitch?* Carol had taken off her glasses and was squinting at the screen, her top lip peeled up from her teeth, the lower lip hanging open.

When Jenna got out of the car at the beach house, she was certain she had a fever. The air and the sand and the sea were all the same visible material, all of it blowing slowly around her as she swayed. Hadn't Bill and Hillary and Chelsea gone to a seaside, to Hilton Head, or a destination like it, after the Monica story broke? Could it be that the Carolinas were the universal place to hang your head, the place for consolation? Whichever vacation spot, it was the ocean, the salt, the surf, the endless whump-whump of the waves, that with some luck could reduce human experience to nothing.

She was not prepared for Sally's first words to her as they embraced on the front porch. "Are you all right?"

Jenna startled in her arms.

"I'm assuming it wasn't for real," Sally went on, pulling Jenna closer to her.

Mrs. Voden let out a mouselike squeak into her hostess's ear. She blamed herself for being taken in by evil. It did not seem too strong a word to her, evil, evil dressed so simply, so beautifully, bland as flummery. Although she knew she was responsible, she was not past wanting to strangle Laura Rider, and in that moment she could have done it quickly, efficiently. Had Sally signed up for the newsletter in the Prairie Wind guest book that had been next to the cash register the day they'd visited? Or had every person in the United States of America been sent the e-mail? Jenna was not sure if she could kill Charlie at this juncture. She would be filled with grief if he was murdered, a fact that made her plight seem doubly pathetic. "Did Dickie see it?" Jenna whimpered.

"Sweetheart!" Frank cried to Sally, coming up the path from the car. Sally, now in Frank's arms, looked over his shoulder at Jenna, asking, with her enormous blue eyes, the next obvious question. No, Frank had not heard the news. Jenna shuddered in answer to her friend. She had seven days in the sun to let her husband know how she, Every Woman, had fallen.

# Chapter 17

FOR LAURA, LATE AUGUST AND EARLY SEPTEMBER WERE ONE continuous high. For starters, there was the *Jenna Faroli Show,* a peak experience. Although she knew she hadn't registered all of it as it was happening, she was afraid to listen to it online, afraid to disturb the afterglow. She knew there would come a moment in her writing life when she'd need a boost, and it was then that she would turn to the Milwaukee Public Radio Web site for a shot in the arm. Many of her customers had heard the show, and in the weeks after the program they said they were interested to read her book when she was finished with it. Not one person mentioned the newsletter, maybe because it was no better than spam and went straight into the trash, or perhaps the *insert* hadn't made sense and so why bother commenting? Or, maybe Laura's clientele admired her for her ability to have fun with someone important and they were in awe, or else the silence was a matter of politeness. It was hard to say. In any case, for the first time in her life, Laura seemed to have cachet with the ladies of Hartley.

And then, as if all that support weren't enough, over Labor Day she'd gone to the Wisconsin Dells, to the Bear Claw Resort and Conference Center, which turned out, amazingly, to be an even higher peak experience than the *Jenna Faroli Show.* She'd been mistakenly put into the literary workshop, instead of romance, a disappointment at first. The romance teacher, Wanda Carol Newman, was so vibrant and full of excitement, and she clutched her Bear Claw clipboard to her chest, and her charges followed behind her as if she were Mother Goose. Laura said to the workshop director, "Do I have to go to Literary?" The director had assured her that she'd love it, and that if she conquered Literary, if she learned about character and setting and lyrical language and punctuation, which was Literary in a nutshell, she could hang all that expertise on any plot that occurred to her.

The Literary person, Valerie Shippell, looked as anyone might have expected: short, thin, but with a menopausal paunch, nondescript hair, and small oval glasses that were only slightly larger than her beige eyes. She'd apparently written several books that had not, as far as Laura could tell, been read by class members, or anyone else, for that matter. The books were critically acclaimed, it said in the brochure, but, as it happened, they were out of print.

The Bear Claw Resort was an ideal location, because if you

were outdoorsy you could hike the trails along the Wisconsin River, but if you weren't that type there was a water park inside the hotel, including a one-thousand-gallon tipping bucket, and the Howlin' Tornado, advertised as a "6 story funnel of outrageous tubin'." Their teacher, Valerie, said that the muffled shrieks of the children and adults alike from inside the enormous fiberglass structure made it sound as if they were being tortured, as if their suffering were being suppressed. But, then, that, as Laura learned, was the way Valerie thought: evil, discontent, discouragement around every corner. And even though Valerie's assessment that the resort was tacky was true, it was tacky in an expensive, rough-hewn way which Laura did not find all that offensive. She had never been happier than in her room with a log-cabin motif, with a loft for the bed, so that when she woke she looked out, not to the parking lot and the Home Depot across the street, but instead to the woods in the distance.

There were ten others in Literary. In the first several minutes of the class, Laura was intimidated because of the grave, ominous sound of "Literary," but she soon saw that there was nothing to fear in people who were serious, just as she was, about the work. They met in the corner of the Timber Ridge Banquet Hall, at a large round table. You could imagine the place gussied up for a special dinner, folded napkins in towers, and orchid centerpieces, place cards, party favors, rows of cutlery. For now the room was quiet, the fifty tables bare. Scattered through the hall were some of the other groups, including True Crime, Mystery, Thrillers, and Self-Help, but they all seemed far away; they all seemed in a different galaxy. After the introductions, Valerie Shippell told her students to find a silent corner for thirty minutes, and write about something they had never told anyone before. To get their juices, she said, flowing.

Laura had gone down to the grand post-and-beam lobby, four stories high, and she sat by the mammoth fieldstone fireplace in a deep-green-and-black plaid chair. It was not exactly silent, but under the massive yellow beams holding up the place, and the vaulted ceiling, she felt as if she were in a cathedral, as if she were about to engage in a holy contemplation. A deep calm filled her. As she sat, eyes closed, she considered writing about the Jenna Faroli newsletter episode, but in a way that was not fulfilling the assignment, since potentially a lot of people, 637 to be exact, knew about the gaffe.

On that Thursday, she had driven home from the *Jenna Faroli Show* without seeing the road, the stop signs, the landmarks, the blue sky. She could not see anything but her own glittering future. It had not been possible to thank Jenna personally after the program, because the next guest had been brought into Studio B even before Laura's segment was finished. Jenna had not had a second to turn to her to say goodbye, but Laura understood. The host had to gather up her generosity and let it shower down upon the next author. Ms. Faroli had boosted Laura's self-esteem to the stratosphere, and in effect given Laura permission to start writing. Laura figured she'd send her an e-mail when she got home. What a concept, writing to Jenna as Laura Patricia Rider, writing to Jenna as herself.

Charlie had been waiting for her in the kitchen, with a copy of the newsletter, rolled up in a tube, in his fist. It was funny, she later thought, that he was the one who was angry, when the Jenna message proved that he was the guilty party. It was Laura who should have been livid. It was Laura who, by all rights, should have claimed the moment.

"What? What"—Charlie was huffing—"are we, are we supposed to do about this?" He was waving the tube at her. He was so rarely in a temper that the spectacle of him, his face gone pink and puffy, his shortness of breath, was unnerving.

"What are you talking about?" She had just had her triumph. What could be wrong? Couldn't she rest on her laurels for one instant before whatever the next crisis was?

"How many people?" he spat, "does the newsletter go out to?"

"I don't know. Six hundred and thirty-seven?"

He slapped the tube into her hand so hard her fingers smarted.

"What's the matter," she said, unrolling the pages, "with—with . . ."

"You—you're laughing?" He was goggle-eyed. "All you can do is laugh?"

She couldn't help it. Oh my God! She had no memory of having done such a thing, but she did recall how lightheaded and exhausted and wound up she'd been the night before. "Charlie," she said through her snickers but trying really as hard as she could not to laugh, "I didn't mean to—"

"Didn't mean to?" He was shouting at her. "How do you think Jenna will feel? I've been trying to reach her. Do you understand how, how—"

"Just a minute," Laura snapped. "Hold on here. Let's get a few things straight. Mrs. Voden shouldn't have written the message in the first place. Did you ever think about that? Not that I meant to paste it in there"—she snorted, the laughter coming through her nose—"because I didn't."

"Stop laughing!"

"I'm trying, I am."

"It's not funny."

"Okay, okay."

"Did Jenna read this before the show? Did she know?"

"You heard her." Laura ate a grape from the fruit bowl. "She was amazing. She was fantastic. She wanted to talk about me, about my dreams, about my real work, instead of gardening. She was unbelievably—"

"That's her," he said, shaking his head. "That's how she is." Charlie, standing by the sink, looked as if he was about to cry, as if he might turn around and bend over the drain in order that his tears not drench his clothing or the floor. "That's totally who she is." His voice was cracking. "And no, I didn't catch the program. I had to help José with the mower, and I missed it." Laura ate another grape, and another. "And by the way," he said, angry again, "my mother called this morning. She called to ask what was going on, what kind of joke we were playing."

Mrs. Rider sank into the chair. Even though she truly hadn't meant to paste Jenna's message into the newsletter, she all at once realized what she'd done: this was it. This was the Black Moment for her lovers. It had finally arrived. They were exposed in the most unflattering light, exposed as the perverted, shallow, obsessed sex-maniacs that they were. And so here was the question: how were they going to get through it to reclaim their best selves? A woman still wants a man to show her who she is, and maybe in some way Charlie had done that for Jenna. Laura was going to have to get to her study to figure it out, to work through the problem.

"I'm not denying," she said, "that this is a weird and upsetting situation." Jenna Faroli was the kindest person Laura had ever met. Everyone in the world read e-mails first thing in the morning, so it was certain that Jenna had seen the newsletter. And still she had treated Laura like an artist. Hadn't she? If there was a small speck of doubt, the memory of Jenna's big mouth and sharp teeth as she chopped through her words in the last few seconds of the interview, Laura let it float beyond her sight line. No, Jenna had spoken to Laura as if she'd seen exactly who she was. Maybe, just maybe, her generosity to Laura was not only a result of Jenna's special vision but also a way to repay Laura for the gift of Charlie. "Maybe," she ventured, "maybe the newsletter doesn't seem like such a big deal to Jenna?"

"Are you crazy?" Charlie cried. "Not a big deal?" He picked up a kitchen chair and threw it to the floor. "You have wrecked her life, do you hear me? And you've destroyed our lives, too."

Laura wasn't sure if he meant she'd destroyed the Riders' lives, or if she'd ruined Jenna and Charlie's cozy arrangement.

In the lobby of the Bear Claw Resort, it took Laura several minutes to decide that she should write about the death of her father rather than the Jenna Faroli newsletter incident. The murder of her father by her mother, her mother allowing her father to choke to death, was a straightforward event, something she could write about in the remaining twenty-five minutes without too much trouble. She was not sorry in her choice, because when she read it out loud to the class in the corner of the Timber Ridge Banquet Hall, she felt that right away she had them in the palm of her hand. She had imagined that she would be much more nervous than she actually was. Once she got going, by the third sentence, she was there with her mother at the kitchen table, watching her father begin to gag on the broccoli stalk. She was there watching her father tip over to the floor. She waited to make sure he was quite dead before placing the phone call. It was as if, in the act of creation, in that neverland, she became her mother.

There was silence at the Literary table when she finished her piece. Laura didn't start shaking until it was over. She had to sit on her hands, bite down hard on her lip, and try, as best she could, to slow her breathing. Valerie Shippell removed her glasses and blew her nose. Her lashes were so light her eyes looked bald, parrotlike in her rhythmic blinking. "That is powerful material," she said to Laura. With those colorless eyes it was difficult to tell that she was actually looking at you. "Good job."

"It must have been healing to write," Nora said. "Here you are, and you've never told anyone this story? That's got to be therapeutic."

Laura guessed it was true. Maybe there was a weight that had been lifted, and yet, at the same time, she was full up with the wonder of the pages she'd written, the wonder of her own words.

"I like the description of his neck, the chicken flesh," Doug said, and Kayla said, "I like the part where the clock ticking is in the wife's heart, that her heart is the clock."

"I love how she just waited," Tawny said, "while the clock ticked, how it ticked softly, how it ticked loud, how it ticked in singsong, and how the ticking echoed inside of her."

"I like," Rhonda said, "how she felt light and lighter as time ticked on. And then how bizarre it was, that she was singing 'Three Blind Mice' to herself."

It was a very heady experience. Laura couldn't ever remember being supported by so many loving people, and that would include her wedding day, when her own sister had tried to sabotage the event. After they had all said what they admired about her piece, Valerie spoke about how Laura, if she wished to hone the scene—and with such powerful material she surely should—might want to focus on concrete details. For instance, the color of the father's face as time wore on. What was the mother doing with her hands while she waited? Laura might want to tone down the imagery of the mother's heart as a clock, which was a bit cumbersome, and think about the sounds the father would have made, the way his chair hit the floor, and how still the room became when he was dead. She should think about the detachment of the narrator, should think if the black humor was intentional, and if it was, she might develop it. Before Laura could say, "Black humor?" Valerie pronounced for the third time that it was extremely powerful material.

"It's incredible," Doug said.

Laura tried to be helpful to the others as they read their pages, but she couldn't help basking inside the shining cloud of her own piece. She'd not only written up a storm, she thought; she'd written the storm itself. When the afternoon was so quickly over, she went, carrying her Bear Claw Resort and Conference Center clipboard with her fresh pad of paper, up to her room to begin the exercises Valerie had assigned.

Even if she hadn't been held aloft by her new friends, even if she hadn't felt by the workshop's end that they understood her essential being in a way that no one, besides Jenna Faroli, had done, she would have been more than happy to get away from home. Together, before she'd left for the Dells, she and Charlie had composed a message to the newsletter list apologizing for the joke. They'd kept it short, because there was no point in drawing more attention to the mistake. Charlie continued to be in a state of agitation, however: Jenna hadn't contacted him since the Laura Show, as he referred to it. He'd been sending his lover e-mails, he'd called her cell, he'd texted her. He knew she was on vacation, but she had assured him that Dickie's beach house was equipped with wireless, and that they'd be able to communicate as usual. Laura had written to her also, and gotten no response. Over Labor Day, Charlie was calling his wife at the Bear Claw Resort every half-hour, and when she did answer she tried to reassure him, telling him that on the Outer Banks there might not be cellphone service, and that the promise of wireless could have been false advertising. She reminded him that Jenna would never have been so openhearted if she'd been upset about the newsletter.

One of the things that still incensed Charlie was the fact that he'd never been able to tell Jenna about his experience with the Silver People. He'd never had the chance to relate what had happened in his own words. He'd been working up to it, crafting the story in his mind. If there was anything that aggravated him about his wife, in addition to her stupendous faux pas, it was how she'd stolen the story, *his* story, out from under him, especially when Jenna had charged him with telling it as well as he knew how. He wanted to make contact with Jenna—he needed to reach her—so that he'd know that she was all right. He also wanted to find out if they were finished. Never again meet in the Kewaskum Inn? He must tell her, once more, just how much he loved her.

He wondered if there was any good that could come from the newsletter incident and from his isolation from Mrs. Voden. Laura had gone off to the Dells to do a writing workshop, to pursue a hobby she'd always dreamed of, which was news to Charlie. Maybe, just maybe, he'd sit himself down in his nook, in the odd silence of the creaky farmhouse. Maybe he'd write, too, why not? He'd take up paper and ballpoint pen, go the old-fashioned route. He'd write to his muse using his "narrative skills," as she had called them, so that she would believe his story, his truth, that one night, long ago, he was carried away.

On the second day of the workshop, they went around the table and talked about what books they were working on or hoping to write. Although the others in the group had purposefully signed up for Literary, their projects sounded like normal books. Kayla was writing a love story about a real-estate agent and a client, but then the client turns out to have been fathered by the same sperm donor as the real-estate agent, which they don't realize until the morning of the wedding. Talk about a Black Moment. At the end, the hero pledges to devote himself to genetic engineering so that they can have biological children who are shielded by technology from the negatives of intermarriage. Doug was rewriting the Arthurian legend set in New Orleans during Katrina, and Tawny was starting a project about a sex-offender priest who goes to Europe to have both of his hands surgically removed. When it was Laura's turn, she explained that she wanted to write a romance, but a different sort of romance, a novel in which the characters have an elevated consciousness. Jenna had supplied the term—the conscious romance—which Laura was hoping might be a whole new subgenre.

While Laura had the floor, Valerie looked up into the face of the stuffed bear that hung over the dais. Right into his fanged mouth. "A conscious romance," she repeated, as if to herself. "That sounds like an oxymoron to me." She tilted her bland face to give the bear a different angle of herself. "Can falling in love be a conscious experience? If it were, that would change the nature of love." She turned to her students. "Love is savage, people. Sexual love blows apart your assumptions, your sense of self, your place in the world. It's a hurricane—it's a nuclear bomb. Don't kid yourself that Eros is a cute little winged angel with a rubber arrow. That arrow will . . . kill."

For the next fifteen minutes, and Laura was not exaggerating when she recounted to her classmates what they'd each experienced, for fifteen minutes Valerie couldn't stop talking about love as insanity, and about the hope that romantic love promises, only to let down those who believe. She recited:

"For each ecstatic instant
We must an anguish pay
In keen and quivering ratio
To the ecstasy."

Laura, of course, would never say, but maybe there were other reasons Valerie had been disappointed by love besides being taken in by a pipe dream. But this, clearly, was Literary, nothing but negativity, nothing but pessimism. Valerie herself said so, going on and on about how it was in finely crafted novels that characters lived deeply with sorrow or they lived ambivalently with happiness. Life in great literature, she explained, was nuanced and complex and ambiguous, qualities not usually found in the genres. She asked the students if they didn't think probing a relationship often revealed hostility. She asked them to consider life as shipwreck, and she demanded that when they go home they read Chekhov.

Laura could sort of see what her teacher meant if she made the huge effort to be depressed. She did remember the first time she'd felt the kind of black tunnel of hopelessness Valerie was maybe talking about. She'd been twelve, old for a flower girl, but a flower girl nonetheless. She'd stood in the doorway of the bride's room in the church basement, watching the bridesmaids help her cousin Jersey sit on the toilet. Jersey, it turned out, could not go to the bathroom in the wedding dress by herself. It seemed a strange and terrible world of intimacy that somehow was related to marriage, and it had made Laura feel empty and frightened.

She raised her hand after Valerie was finished talking and said, "I think I know what you're saying, about how life has its secret and black places. But that's not what I want to see in a book or movie. I want a lesson learned. Gratitude and understanding. A healing hand. I like books where people get what they deserve."

Laura wouldn't point out the obvious, the fact that Valerie's books were out of print, the fact that if Valerie could torque her worldview maybe she'd sell a few more copies.

"Take, for example," Laura said, "a situation where a brilliant woman, a genius, is found out for having an affair with a laborer, a simple stonemason. I'd like to see what she learns from that experience. It seems like she could be a better person for it, that there should be a take-home message. In high school we learned about tragedy, how there's supposed to be evil, and then suffering, but finally values. A meaningful man in action. I don't want my heroine to offer herself to the world, to reach with both hands, and what she discovers is that life is awful. What's the point of that?"

Valerie said, "What has compelled your character to take up with a laborer, someone out of her class? Does she feel liberated, or is she ashamed? Will she be punished? Those are certainly some avenues to explore with your plot."

"Punished?" Laura asked. "Punished for being in love? Punished for connecting to her humanity? Punished for being who she is? The stonemason might make her realize that her retarded brother is a complete human being. Maybe the stonemason teaches her to respect her mother, who has Alzheimer's."

Valerie nodded and then lined up her pencils above her clipboard. "I don't know about the rest of you," she said, "but I'm ready for a drink."

The magical aspect of the group was how quickly they got close. They did as Valerie said and adjourned to the bar, and after they were lubed, many of them got their suits and reconvened in the indoor water park. Valerie had a staff meeting, which for Laura, frankly, was a relief. Without their leader, they went down the slides, they played in the interactive treehouse water fort, they went in the Howlin' Tornado, and they took turns soaking in the hot tub. Through all of it, they never stopped talking about writing. Laura admitted that when she read a book she always located the end of the chapter, and each time she turned a page she mentally counted how many more to the finish. She was quick to say it was a habit she hoped to break. Doug, sitting on the edge of the hot tub, announced that he had found a metaphor in the water slide. "So," he said, "you're going through the long tunnel, and the water is both mental juices and amniotic fluid, and when you burst out at the end, it's the birth of an artist. The birth of an artist at Bear Claw Resort. The lifeguard is there in the shallow water, the girl in the red suit holding the safety strap, there for your delivery, and ready to save you if you need it." They all had to laugh at the idea of dowdy, morose Valerie in her tank suit waiting to rescue them.

It wasn't all fun, not by a long shot. Laura worked as hard as she ever had in her life. They had assignments through the day and homework in the evening. She wrote an opening page that Valerie sent her back to rewrite, not once, not twice, but three times. She wrote descriptions of her characters not because she knew exactly who they were, but because Valerie had instructed them to come up with something, to get anything at all on paper. She worked on a sketch about the farm, she rewrote her father's death scene, and she even turned in a short piece about the Knees. She tried a love scene in a hotel room that's interrupted several times by a cell phone, and another few pages, which Valerie praised, about an ugly woman falling in love. Mrs. Rider was definitely starting to hear the mermaids sing. Even if Valerie didn't write interesting books, even if she had a jaundiced outlook, Laura admitted by the end that she was a good taskmaster.

On the last day, she exchanged e-mail addresses with her fellow workshoppers. Doug was going to set up a Bear Claw Resort and Conference Center Literary chat room so they could continue to share their manuscripts, so at least they'd have a virtual community. "None of us will ever be lonely," Nora said. And they would all keep each other posted when they got published. They checked out, they hugged, they waved. When it was really over, Laura sat in the parking lot and cried.

Charlie had still not heard from Jenna when his wife got back from the Dells. "I need to know she's all right," he whined.

Laura didn't say that Jenna was probably just fine without his concern. "She'll get in touch when she has a minute," she said.

"She's furious," Charlie insisted. "She's devastated."

Maybe, Laura thought, Charlie privately subscribed to the Valerie Shippell school of thought, always assuming that people deep down are ravaged. Though Laura had tried to imagine Jenna on the beaches of North Carolina, she had not, because of her own exhilaration, focused on the possible varieties of her idol's suffering, if, indeed, Jenna was unhappy. She had not pictured Jenna taking long walks at dawn by herself, the early hour of that exercise not born from a wish to comb the beach for treasure, but the result of never having fallen asleep.

On the first morning, before Frank and Sally were up, Jenna had talked to Dickie by the water's edge. Her friend had never disappointed her before, and she found it hard to believe, even as it was happening, that he was so uninterested in her humiliation. She did not know if his recent spate of migraines had made spiritual and emotional pain seem insignificant. "No one cares about adultery anymore," he pronounced. "It's unfortunate, the perception in the culture that passionate love no longer has the power to transform. And the end of shame means the novelist no longer has a subject. The novel will die as a result."

Jenna didn't care about the death of the novel. "Dickie!" she cried. "I'm ruined."

"My darling, you are not ruined. I'm sorry to disappoint you, but no one is ruined by this kind of scandal. On the contrary, your stock is probably soaring." And if she was ruined, time would pass, he assured her, the wounds would heal, all would be forgotten, all was vanity, all was dust. The world was coming to an end, and if she had enjoyed herself before the coasts fell into the ocean and Wisconsin became a desert, then she'd done the universe a favor. If she'd enjoyed herself before the jihadists or the Christian Right destroyed Western civilization, she had done well.

She wondered if he was on new medication. She could not explain to him that something fundamental was lost to her, an old-fashioned respect and authority that had seemed part of her nature—*Reputation, reputation, reputation! O, I have lost my reputation! I have lost the immortal part of myself, and what remains is bestial.* And it wasn't only the discovery but the fact that the poison pen had been her own. Sally seemed not to have shared the message with him, and Jenna was too mortified to recite it, but if she had, surely he would have better understood her plight. Because he paid no attention to the technological world, because he'd never used a computer, he did not realize the pandemic speed with which a person's shame could travel. The stain on her honor was bright and indelible. She couldn't bear to think about the amount of energy she'd have to muster to walk out of the door every single day, head held high, from here on out.

*I imagine you are down the hall, and the nurse will wheel me, poor old Jenna Faroli, to Charlie Rider's room in the evening. . . .*

If Dickie had given her any comfort, it was that the end of the world was nigh.

Laura also didn't imagine Jenna's second morning, the moment when Frank was finally settled on the deck with his book, the moment Jenna went out to speak to him. She put a cold glass of tea by his side, and she said, "I'd like to tell you about something."

He shut his novel and closed his eyes, and she knew then that Sally had mentioned the message to him. It did not surprise her. He and Sally had always loved each other, a fact that was clarified for her in that instant. Earlier, the two of them had strolled down the beach, full of their intimacies, amiably knocking into each other, Sally telling Frank what was Jenna's to reveal.

She sat down next to him, brushing away her tears, but he, instead of waiting for her to begin, stood up. He put his hands on her shoulders and, leaning down, chin on her head, spoke over her, into the brushy growth past the deck. "I don't want to hear about it. I'd rather you never said a word to me about the matter."

It was of little consequence that she stifled her sob. He

was gone before she could reach for his hand, back through the glass door, back to his dear friend. There was no one to hear her. She moaned into her lap, "Don't leave me to myself, Frank." When she lifted her head she could see him calmly pouring coffee as if nothing had occurred. "Frank!" There was no one in the world for her now, nothing to do but go down the stairs toward the ocean, toward the morning light, already sharp and glinting on the waves.

Laura didn't imagine Jenna stumbling along the beach, pausing to fish her phone from her pocket, to answer Vanessa's call. Jenna had to kneel in the sand, holding the phone away from her face as Vanessa chattered. She knew that when she saw Charlie at home, in Hartley, she would not recognize him. Not only would she blot out the joy of their Kewaskum Inn afternoons, but she would not understand why he had thrilled her. "Mom," her daughter said, "are you there?" She would no longer believe in delight. "Mom?" Vanessa shouted. "It sounds like someone's being strangled."

Jenna hung up. She weaved along the dry sand and the wet sand as the phone, in her clutches, vibrated.

⌒

It wasn't that Laura had stopped thinking about Jenna, not at all. She wondered, for instance, if most women truly wanted children, if mothering was how they would wish to spend their lives if they were given enough guidance. Jenna was uppermost on her mind on this subject because it did seem that Vanessa was a continuous pain in the neck to her mother. Laura could imagine the stimulation, and maybe even comfort, Jenna took from having a brainy husband, how, back when Jenna was feeding the baby, the judge would talk to her soothingly of case law and listen to her worries. Laura was certain that Judge Voden, the old baldy, hung on his wife's every word. It did occur to her that if Jenna were to disgrace herself in any way, the judge, having seen the gamut of human conduct, would hardly bat an eye. So, if Laura wasn't envisioning the particulars of Jenna's vacation, she was nonetheless mulling over ideas and questions that for her started with Jenna Faroli.

The list of what women wanted was growing longer and more complicated the more she thought about it. The first rule of thumb, though—and this wasn't a bad thing:

1. What women wanted was always in flux. There was always something more, something new, something different to want. In her twenties, for example, Every Woman wanted to couple, to share, and if she was successful in that department, she wanted, by the time she was forty, to be left alone to watch Comedy Central.

2. She did want to be the right woman for her man, easier said than done, but still, a goal. It was sad if the situation arose that she irritated him, belittled him, or henpecked him. Because she absolutely wanted to honor who he was.

3. She wanted dominion in specific areas but with the knowledge that if she was way off course he would steer her straight without ever bragging about or even acknowledging his superior navigation abilities.

4. She wanted a respectful and attentive and sympathetic audience, a man with advanced listening skills but not so advanced he seemed like a phony or a girlfriend. His skills were male, his own, and empowering.

5. She wanted genuine appreciation for her creativity, her flexibility, and her generosity. In addition, she wanted genuine appreciation for her own genuine appreciation for his talents.

6. When it turned out that he had very few of the qualities on the wish list, and if the Serenity Prayer didn't work, that old saw about accepting the things you cannot change, then women wanted the perils of freedom.

Laura wasn't saying that all of the above for both parties didn't take a mind-boggling amount of dedication, generosity, forgiveness, and consciousness. Of course, some women could think of nothing but Mr. Right, some women made bad choice after bad choice, and others wanted to spend their lives wallowing in their yearning. Laura was above all of that wasted energy, in part, she admitted, because maybe she did have a man in her life who was now pretty much calibrated exquisitely. Maybe the whole point of love was to break each other so that from those shattered selves you could build a better, a sturdier self, so that you could go forward—not hand in hand but a comfortable arm's length apart. Ideally, if both parties were conscious in the romance, Every Man and Every Woman would enter the relationship with arms spread wide open, ready for the adventure of being broken to pieces and reassembled. As Laura wrote her book, she was going to be looking both within and down upon the plain of millions of seekers, millions of women, and she was, she hoped, going to teach them what to wish for. Jenna was right, that there was a lot to absorb, the whole long history of womanhood, from Queen Nefertiti to Britney Spears. It did occur to her that maybe she, Laura Rider, was possibly the heroine of the story.

As for Charlie, if Mrs. Voden was truly moving on to greener pastures, he would mope for a while. The shine had gone out of his eyes, but he was keeping busy up in his nook, probably online with his alien support group. Charlie's great blessing was the fact that he was constitutionally incapable of being unhappy for too long. If Jenna had stopped calling, because, maybe, after all, the newsletter thing had gotten to her, if she was worried about her reputation, worried about the People of Hartley, she should let that trouble go. Everyone thought Charlie was a homo. They were probably convinced that if he was going to run off with anyone it was the illegal immigrants who kept Prairie Wind Farm afloat. Charlie was the Ideal Cover for Every Woman who wanted a roll in the hay, the hero who could fake out the community.

After Laura had unpacked from the workshop, she went into her study and sat down at her desk. Before dinner was as good a time as any to get started. She turned on her computer. She'd begin her book using what she'd generated at the Bear Claw Resort, and see what happened. Right off, in her new ergonomic task chair, she felt balanced. She felt ready for what lay ahead. She could see past the screen into the distance. Far off was a hotel ballroom filled with women in gowns, and as she focused she could see herself in a satin bodice with a tulle skirt, up on the dais with authors such as Wanda Carol Newman. Just as she'd known she'd marry lovely, funny, dear Charlie and acquire a beautiful farm, this vision, too, had the sheen of hard work and inevitability. It was real, it was solid, it was true. There she was at the convention of romance readers and writers, a celebration of new talent, an evening with dancing and toasts and champagne and an enormous sheet cake decorated to look like Laura Rider's book jacket. She might not say it out loud, but as she moved to the podium—careful to gather up her voluminous skirt—as she flowed to the mike to describe her writing journey, she would inwardly thank those who had helped her, the Bear Claw group, her husband, and, maybe most of all, Jenna Faroli.

She wasn't averse to having her characters be part of a TV series or a computer game, as Jenna had suggested. The world was changing—humanity itself, perhaps, was changing. There were so many new doorways, doorways upon doorways that opened into story after story. Maybe the creative process wasn't so different from being lifted up in the dark and guided into one bright realm after another. Although she had only begun to ask the questions about Every Woman, it was through her art that she'd find the answers. She crossed her arms over her chest, leaned back in her chair, closed her eyes, and said, "Take me."

# Reading Group Guide

# Discussion Questions

1. Laura muses that "she could only be her ultimate self when she was alone." She isn't the only one who has a clear "real" self and a constructed self. In what ways do the characters create new personas? Are these personalities convincing? Are they necessary?

2. Does Laura have the talent to be a writer? Are there rules that writers must follow, as she believes? Is Jenna correct when she suggests that it's impossible to write without a historical knowledge of what has come before you?

3. How does the first interaction between Charlie and Jenna at the side of the road set the tone for their relationship? What changes and what remains the same once Laura is involved?

4. It is made clear during her interview with Jenna and again at the writers' conference that Laura is not terribly knowledgeable about books and writing. Was she also naïve to involve her husband with another woman? What other characters display inexperience or ignorance?

5. Charlie and Laura are similar to Jenna and Frank in that both couples' passion for one another has cooled after years of marriage. In what other ways are the couples similar? How are they different?

6. How has e-mail affected correspondence? How has it affected writing in general? What opinions would Charlie, Laura, and Jenna each have on the topic?

7. When Charlie thinks back to his childhood and his life with Laura, he recognizes that Prairie Wind Farm "had never been his goal, in part because he'd never had any particular goals." If not his job, what else drives Charlie? What other examples are there of the gap between desire and reality?

8. Is a "conscious romance" possible? What kind of relationship would that be like?

9. Is it possible that Laura did, in fact, mean to paste Jenna's e-mail, whether Laura realizes it consciously or not? Why would she have done it intentionally? Why is her reaction to the e-mail being sent out so different from Charlie's and Jenna's reactions?

10. Laura Rider starts a list of what women want. What would be on your list?

11. Who, in the end, has the upper hand in the Jenna Faroli Radio Show interview with Laura Rider? Or do neither or both have the upper hand?

12. Is any character responsible for Jenna and Charlie's affair? Who or what would be the cause according to Laura? Jenna? Charlie?

13. What is the attraction, either romantic or not, between Charlie, Laura, and Jenna? What does each of them provide to each of the others?

14. In this satire, are all the characters skewered equally?

15. What does Hamilton seem to be saying about the writing life? Are writers necessarily ruthless?

# Q & A with Jane Hamilton

Q: Have you encountered any Laura Riders who misunderstand and/or underestimate what it means to be a writer?

A: Through the years I've encountered her now and again, including she as me! Sometimes I'm awoken in the night by a bolt of such a beautiful idea, and I think, *That will be easy.* The book is all there before me, including the jacket, including the typeface. *I'll just do that tomorrow*, I think. In the light of day, of course, everything becomes complicated, difficult, and usually completely impossible. I usually don't understand the difficulty of a novel until I'm in the middle of it—when I start feeling certain that I'm not up to the task. I think if a writer realized what she was in for at the start of a project she might decide to change careers.

Q: Do any of Jenna's thoughts during her interview with Laura reflect your own?

A: I tend in general to think that any person who wants to make art should study the forms and the history of their genre, not necessarily in the academy, but the writer or painter will be well served to read wildly, wander through museums, etc. I don't think I'm as . . . severe as Jenna. And I believe that Laura Rider has a point, too: that we all have stories to tell. One of the thrills of being a teacher through the years is seeing who comes through—who does the magnificent thing. You can't predict who will really pull off the great stunt of a novel. I think, contrary to Jenna's stern put-down of Laura, that Laura might very well write a capable romance. She certainly knows how to work, and how to research. Like Jenna, however, if hell turns out to be full of amateur musicians, it will indeed, to me, be hellish.

Q: Just as Laura feels that she "knows" Jenna from listening to her radio show, do your readers feel they have an appreciation of (or even a relationship with) you from your books? Do you feel it is possible to understand a person with only an exposure to his or her creative works?

A: I always think it's a potential disappointment to meet writers if you love their work. I myself have had that experience a few times, feeling so thrilled to meet someone I revere, and then they turn out to be sullen, rude, unkind. They are having a bad day, a bad year. But the work, I remind myself, separate from the writer, is still there, shining and pure. Still lovable. Maybe that's a perk of being a writer—you can deflect from yourself by saying, *Wait, but look at the work, it's so much better, more generous, more careful, than I am.* I'd hate to think that someone understands me, the person from my novels—that is to say, what is it they understand? No, don't tell me! I don't want to know!

Q: What spurred you to write a comedic novel? Was writing *Laura Rider's Masterpiece* a different experience from writing your past novels?

A: I was so blue about the way print culture is going, and I'd had some interesting students in a workshop, people who wanted to write but didn't seem to love reading or books, and I was filled with doubt about writing serious character-driven novels, that the only thing I could think to do was try to amuse myself, to try to make myself laugh, to take a stab at what is so strange and funny about writing books at this moment in American culture.

   The book turned out to be a joy to write—a story that came in one puff, that wrote itself. For me comedy is either there, or it's not there—that is, there's no use in straining to try to make something funny. Comedy, it seems to me, is a gift from the cosmos. Of course you can't know if someone else will find the work funny, but it made me laugh every day, and I'm grateful for that.

Q: This story is a cautionary tale regarding love in the time of the Internet. How do you feel about e-mail, blogs, and how they and other online features have changed communication?

A: E-mail, so scary! How many times have I pressed SEND only to feel my blood go icy. WHOOPS! Everything is sped up now (although, who knows, maybe in the time of Jane Austen, with three mail deliveries a day, a romance could progress fairly quickly). With e-mail you can meet, fall in love, have sex, and break up in the space of about a day. What's missing, to my sensibility, is savoring the experience. Taking out the letter from your purse and reading it, and sniffing it, and reading it again, and rereading it once more. There's no better satisfaction than love on paper with ink.

Q: What do you think it is about romances that appeals to women, both in reading and writing them? Do you agree with Laura that women are looking for heroes with a feminine tenderness?

A: A good romance is about coming both to self-knowledge and a deep understanding of the beloved. That's why we still read Jane Austen, why the union of Mr. Darcy and Elizabeth Bennet is such a satisfying marriage: both of them have seen the other's most woeful flaws and sterling qualities. Add to that their youth, their beauty, Darcy's wealth—the next generation is going to be even smarter, more beautiful, wiser, better, and undoubtedly richer! I think at a deep level we read romances because we love to think of the world growing more beautiful through beautiful unions.

I do think the heroes in many romances, as Laura notes, develop their feminine sides *after* being educated by the forbearing heroine. The men often begin as brutish lugs and become sensitive human beings.

Q: Why did you include the Emily Dickinson poem that Valerie Shippell recited to her students ("For each ecstatic instant / We must an anguish pay / In keen and quivering ratio / To the ecstasy," page 203)? Do you think that Dickinson's characterization of love is accurate?

A: Valerie is determined that her students understand that *life is suffering!* And that *suffering* is the theme of *literature.* What better poem to illustrate that than Emily Dickinson's lines? People who have died of AIDS and the legions who've died of venereal disease might, in particular, have said that Dickinson nailed it. It's a bitter pill to swallow, to be sure. I do wonder what experience Dickinson had that propelled her to write those lines.

Q: It's impossible for writers to pinpoint where their ideas come from, but do you ever find yourself influenced by real life, as Laura Rider was? Similarly, do your stories ever follow you into the real world and affect your interactions with other people (perhaps to disastrous results)?

A: I am influenced by real life at every turn (but then the fun is to whack up real life, turn it upside down, inside out). If my stories ever follow me into real life, I will try to run away very, very fast.

Q: What writers do you look to for inspiration? Were there any you turned to in particular in writing this satire?

A: I read Evelyn Waugh's *A Handful of Dust,* and Jane Austen especially. I wanted to write a short book that was all about narrative thrust, as well as making fun of the point we've landed ourselves in the culture just now, and both Waugh and Austen were the perfect teachers.

Q: When/how did you know that writing was your calling? Did you find that you needed both courage, as Laura would attest, and research, as Jenna would emphasize? Do you have any advice for those looking to write?

A: I always loved to be by myself in my own world—that's what writing was for me. But I never imagined that my work would be published. I'm not sure it takes courage to write something if it's going to be private, but sometimes it takes starch to imagine other people reading the work. You may well feel exposed, and you know you'll be judged. It takes a lot of courage, for example, to go on Amazon and read the reviews. Research is a wonderful part of the process, a time when you can justify spending hours and hours learning about all kinds of things, and at the same time the story is coming into focus.